Praise for t

"The Galliano Club series promises to be as riveting as Amato's previous novels set in Mexico. The Roaring Twenties in their uninhibited violence and excitement come alive . . . A sure hit with loyal fans and new readers alike."

Michael Hogan, author of *Women of the Irish Rising*

"A gripping thriller series that will immerse you in the gritty, violent world of America in the 1920s. Clawing their way through the tale are a host of desperate characters that will shock and amaze you, never allowing you to catch your breath until the jaw-dropping conclusion."

Amanda Hughes, author of *The Looking Glass Goddess* and *The Image Seeker*

"Spot-on historic atmosphere as the compelling characters fight, dance, and gamble their way to the Galliano Club . . . An epic tale with all the glitz, danger and gritty charm of the era."

L.A. Chandlar, award-winning author of the Art Deco Mystery Series

"An exciting storyline, mob violence and intense characters."

Elizabeth Martina, author of the Hadley Sisters mystery series

"A keen eye for period detail while not overlooking timeless human traits. Greed, loss, love, and loyalty play equal parts . . . Lovers of the Roaring Twenties, The Godfather trilogy, or underdog stories should find much to like here.

Bradley Harper, author of award-winning novels *A Knife in the Fog*, and *Queen's Gambit*

Also by Carmen Amato

DETECTIVE EMILIA CRUZ SERIES

CLIFF DIVER: Detective Emilia Cruz Book 1

HAT DANCE: Detective Emilia Cruz Book 2

DIABLO NIGHTS: Detective Emilia Cruz Book 3

KING PESO: Detective Emilia Cruz Book 4

PACIFIC REAPER: Detective Emilia Cruz Book 5

43 MISSING: Detective Emilia Cruz Book 6

RUSSIAN MOJITO: Detective Emilia Cruz Book 7

NARCO NOIR: Detective Emilia Cruz Book 8

MADE IN ACAPULCO: The Emilia Cruz Stories

THE ARTIST/EL ARTISTA: A Bilingual Short Story

FELIZ NAVIDAD FROM ACAPULCO: A Detective Emilia Cruz Novella

THE LISTMAKER OF ACAPULCO: A Detective Emilia Cruz Novella

THRILLERS

AWAKENING MACBETH

THE HIDDEN LIGHT OF MEXICO CITY

NON-FICTION (EDITOR)

INSIDER'S GUIDE TO THE BEST OF MEXICO

INSIDER'S GUIDE TO THE BEST OF MEXICAN HOLIDAYS

ROAD TO THE GALLIANO CLUB

prequel to the Galliano Club series

Carmen Amato

COPYRIGHT

Published 2022 by Laurel & Croton
Trade Paperback Edition

Identifiers: ISBN: 978-1-7353079-2-3 (print)
ISBN 978-1-7353079-1-6 (ebook)

ROAD TO THE GALLIANO CLUB

prequel to the Galliano Club series

Carmen Amato

From Italy to Chicago, hard luck forces three unforgettable characters to defy the odds and strike out on their own.

All journeys end at the Galliano Club during Prohibition, where murder, blackmail and revenge are always on tap.

Free refills.

FOREWORD

In the pages ahead, you are going to meet dancer Ruth Cross, bartender Luca Lombardo, and bootlegger Benny Rotolo. Each travels a hard road that ends at the Galliano Club, a social hub for Italian men in the fictional city of Lido, New York, during America's experiment with Prohibition.

Lido is based on my hometown of Rome, New York. When I was growing up, Rome was a close-knit community where almost everyone was Italian, Irish, or Polish, and a Roman Catholic. Five hours north of New York City and the Statue of Liberty, the city was surrounded by dairy farms, with milk delivered to the insulated box on our back porch every day. The backbone of the local economy was Revere Copper and Brass. The big mill turned out tea kettles and ship hulls, earning Rome its "Copper City" nickname.

Spargo Wire and Rome Cable made more things out of metal. Griffiss Air Force Base kept us all safe, with the occasional sonic boom to prove it. Going to Goldberg's or Nelson's department stores with my grandmother was an Event, as was church on Sunday and sleepovers at my cousin Celine's house.

The Fourth of July meant picnics with the extended family. Christmas meant downtown shopping with my sisters and lunch later at the Candyland Restaurant with its tabletop jukeboxes. On wintry mornings, we all shoveled snow before school.

Rome was Mayberry, just colder and more Catholic.

By the time I graduated from high school, I was ready to explore the wider world. I headed off to college in the big city of Syracuse, an hour away. I took the train and saw the Statue of Liberty. I spent my junior year in Paris. Graduate school at the University of Virginia led to a job with the Central Intelligence Agency.

Through the years, every time I visited, Rome had lost another round in the quality-of-life sweepstakes. The commercial district was razed to build an exact replica of Fort Stanwix, the Revolutionary War fort that never surrendered, but the expected influx of tourists never came. New York's high taxes sucked up wages and jobs. The Air Force shuttered the base. Prolonged union strikes led to the closure of major manufacturers. A state facility for the disabled and mentally handicapped became a prison.

I spent a few years working in Mexico. Despite the stress of the drug war that no one seemed to be winning, in this mostly Catholic country where family comes first, I discovered rhythms and values that reminded me of home.

In Mexico, family bonds were formed and strengthened in the kitchen. Community was built around a Catholic church tending its flock, not just with Sunday Mass, but through numerous opportunities to gather. Not everything was instantly available; money was tight for most Mexicans. Necessity led to creativity, just like when I was growing up.

Inducted into Rome's Arts Hall of Fame in 2019, I was asked if I would ever write a mystery about Rome. At the time, I didn't think so.

Now with 10 books set in Mexico under my belt, I'm being tugged back home. Not to present-day Rome, which is still struggling, but to the vibrant city of the 1920's where my grandparents started their family during the height of Prohibition.

None of the characters in the Galliano Club novels are specifically based on either of my grandparents, yet Ann and Joe Sestito inspire every page.

A gifted tailor, Ann's nickname was Sheba, slang for a sexy girl. Joe was an Oneida County deputy sheriff, running the jail in the county courthouse, later working at the Revere Copper and Brass Rolling Mill. He played saxophone in the Liberty Club band.

I grew up in the house next door. Coffee and donuts in their kitchen after Sunday Mass anchored the week. That's when my grandfather could be persuaded to tell stories of Prohibition. Getting kicked by a prisoner so hard it left a permanent dent in his shin. Spending a freezing winter night in a cemetery waiting for bootleggers who'd staged an elaborate funeral for a coffin loaded with booze. The grudge that flamed into murder and a manhunt the day of their wedding reception.

The ledgers Joe kept during his years as Rome's City Marshal, which I still have, provided even more grist for a writer's imagination.

Sincere thanks go to Maria Rich of the Rome Arts Hall of Fame, who planted the seed for the series. I'm grateful for the assistance of Arthur L. Simmons III at the Rome Historical Society and Patrick Reynolds, Director of Public Programs at the Oneida County Historical Society. Thank you to Linda Iannone for a behind-the-scenes private tour of the incomparable Stanley Theatre in Utica.

Last, but not least, my thanks go to James R. Guy, president of the real Galliano Club in Rome. In September 2020, he kindly gave permission to use the Galliano Club name. The 1920 building still stands, smaller than the fictional club, but with the same twin doors and dance studio on the second floor.

Carmen Amato
March 2022

Old sins have long shadows.

Italian proverb

PART 1: RUTH

October 1904

Number 17, Miner's Row
Mahanoy, Pennsylvania

"You start tomorrow at the breakers with the rest of the girls," Ruth's stepfather said. Oblivious to the impact of his announcement, Jed Hogan shoveled stew into his mouth as he hunched over the bowl with his elbows on the table.

Ruth had known this day was coming but it still took her by surprise. "I have school," she said.

"You're sixteen." Jed coughed as he swabbed a piece of bread around his plate to sop up the watery gravy. Despite a wash, his leathery fingers were stained with coal dust, just like the squint lines around his red-rimmed eyes. He coughed again, spraying out soggy crumbs. "Time you earned your keep around here."

Jed constantly hacked up black phlegm. His relentless cough kept everyone in the cramped house awake at night. The doctor at the mining company clinic said it was nothing to worry about.

"If I graduate, I can make twice as much money as a secretary," Ruth pointed out, remembering all the arguments she'd stored up when today inevitably came. "Even more if I get a teaching certificate like Miss Prescott."

Jed spat into his handkerchief, adding another dark stain to it, and spooned up more of his dinner. Francie Hogan shook her head at her daughter as Ruth's three young stepbrothers ignored the conversation, busy bolting their food because there was never quite enough for a family of six. The boys, Jed's children with the wife who killed herself, would be swinging pickaxes with their father in a few short years.

Ruth finished the tasteless stew in her own bowl. If she started working at the mine, she'd be trapped forever just like everyone else in Mahanoy. Working the breakers meant picking leftover coal out of the slag heaps produced by the mine. It was a job usually reserved for boys who were too young for digging coal out of the Pennsylvania hills. Strikes and sabotage had left the company shorthanded, however, so boys were going underground now, too. To fill the gap, the company was now hiring girls to sort through the tailings.

For thirty-five cents a day, breakers spent ten hours in a shack on a wooden bench salvaging bits of coal and inhaling the omnipresent dust. Bent over a steady stream of broken rock as it poured out of a chute, within two or three days every breaker's hands were cut to pieces. Contact with jagged rock and the iron chute wore nails down to the quick. The salvaged bits of coal were invariably flecked with blood.

Unlike her school friends, Ruth's dreams were bigger than back-breaking days covered in coal dust just to live in a company house and buy food at the company store; bigger than marriage to a miner and pumping out more babies than she could feed. When her man died of the black lung or in a pit accident, she'd be expected to marry another, just like her mother.

Ruth wanted new clothes and polished floors and velvet curtains. Francie didn't like it when Ruth talked about music or books or eating in a restaurant. Dismissed the crazy ideas her daughter picked up from trashy magazines, or the no-account carnival people who passed through Mahanoy on the way to places with uppity names. Jed's company house with his dead wife's Blue Willow china was luxury enough for Francie. Her daughter had a Sunday dress, too. Wanting more was a sin.

But Francie had promised Ruth that she could graduate from high school.

"Miss Prescott says I'm good enough to get a job as a dancer," Ruth said doggedly into Jed's silence. "A real dancer in New York City."

"That teacher is no good." Jed scowled and shoved his empty plate away. "All she does is fill your head with crazy talk. Nobody makes money dancing."

Ruth clenched her fists and turned to her mother. "Ma, you heard her say that. You heard her say I was real good."

"Ruthie June Crosswater," Francie said quietly. "Don't go spoiling the man's supper."

"I'm not going to work at the mine," Ruth said to her mother in the same soft tone. "I don't care what he says."

"She starts tomorrow." Jed jabbed a finger across the table at Francie. "You agreed. I don't want to hear any more about it."

"You agreed?" Ruth exclaimed.

Francie looked down, refusing to meet anyone's eye.

"Ma, is he lying?" Ruth could barely breathe. "You promised I could graduate."

Her stepfather leaned across the table and slapped Ruth across the face hard enough to loosen her teeth. Her chair skidded sideways. Ruth caught herself on the edge of the table a second before she toppled to the floor.

"Your mother's got nothing to do with this," Jed roared, the phlegm rattling in his lungs. "You're done with that damn fool school. You start at the breakers tomorrow."

Still seeing stars, Ruth stumbled out of the kitchen. Her mother's duplicity was a sharp, piercing hurt. Her stepbrothers immediately began squabbling over the slice of bread buttered with lard left by her bowl.

Francie stayed at the table, head bent as the boys squabbled and Jed belched. Ruth threw on her coat and fled.

The house was a mining company crackerbox, identical to every other crackerbox in the rows of houses that snaked along the base of the hill below the pithead. The Crosswater family had lived in an identical house two rows over. When Ruth's father Bill died, and the mining company sent an eviction notice, Francie married Jed.

Jed's house wasn't home for Ruth, despite the same footprint. It was crammed with stepbrothers, endless piles of laundry, and unspoken misery. There was no place to hide and lick her wounds.

It was already dark and chilly. Cold gravel crunched under her boots as she ran. Greasy coal oil light shone in the windows of the other row houses as if to illuminate the symphony of coughing that emanated from each residence.

Miss Prescott was at home in the tiny cottage allotted to her by the company-run school board. She was the only person in Mahanoy who lived alone; a forty-something spinster with a perpetually wistful look in her eye. She taught every subject to the high school students, from mathematics to Civil War history, as well as tap dancing lessons in her parlor on Saturday mornings.

"Ruthie!" Miss Prescott wiped her hands on a dishrag as she stood in the doorway, a faded apron over the severe navy dress she wore to school, her ever-present cameo brooch at her throat. "How nice to see you. I was just finishing my supper dishes."

"Can I come in?"

"Of course." Miss Prescott held the door for Ruth, who burst into tears as soon as she stepped into the warmth of the teacher's cozy parlor.

The story came out over cups of weak tea in Miss Prescott's kitchen. "I can't do it," Ruth ended unhappily. "I won't."

"I don't know what to say." Miss Prescott looked close to tears herself.

"I'll run away," Ruth declared. Her voice shook with both sadness and defiance. "If I stay here, I'll be trapped forever."

"Yes, you will." Miss Prescott's voice was barely audible.

Ruth clasped her hands around the teacup, afraid to look at her teacher. Miss Prescott was trapped, too. Just like the miners, she paid rent to the company and bought her food at the company store. The company provided the books and decreed what Miss Prescott could and could not teach.

The Saturday dance classes were tolerated but not encouraged. There were too few students for anyone to really care.

"What should I do?" Ruth asked, trying not to cry again.

"Are you serious, Ruthie?"

Ruth swiped the back of her hand across her eyes. "Yes."

Miss Prescott left the kitchen. Ruth heard a door quietly open and close. When Miss Prescott came back, she handed

Ruth a small pamphlet. It was the schedule of the new bus that ran between Joliet and Hazelton. Mahanoy was one of the stops on the route.

Automobiles were rare in Mahanoy, except for the mine owner's fancy Buick touring car with yellow wheels. The bus was an open air Autocar Tonneau with a flat canvas roof and two rows of benches that could hold eight adults if they didn't mind the squeeze. When the Tonneau passed through, stopping in front of the company store on Main Street, it was always a thrill. Packages and mail came and went this way now, but the real excitement swirled around the passengers. Who got on and who got off was an entire day's worth of gossip for Ruth's mother.

"I don't have the money for a ticket." It was one of Ruth's dreams to get on that Tonneau but dreams cost money. Even if they wanted to, Ruth knew her mother and stepfather could not afford the fare to Hazelton, an hour away, much less what it cost to go all the way to New York City.

"I can give you five dollars, Ruthie," Miss Prescott said. She took a handful of well-worn bills from her apron pocket. "Take it and get out of here. Write me a letter someday and tell me how you made out. Or maybe I'll read about you in the newspaper. All about your big success on Broadway."

Ruth was afraid to take the bills. They lay there on the table, a ticket to the world that meant leaving Francie, leaving Mahanoy, leaving everything Francie knew. Life waited for her out there, but it was a life full of strangers, where Ruth would have only her dreams to show her the way.

"I'll pay you back," Ruth promised as tears welled up again.

The teacher hugged Ruth and they both cried. But it wasn't long until they put their heads together over another pot of tea and made a plan for Ruth's escape.

Ruth walked back to Jed's house with her heart in her throat.

Once her stepbrothers were asleep in the room she shared with them, Ruth layered on every stitch of clothing she had, which wasn't much. Miss Prescott's money went into her coin purse, along with Ruth's personal fortune of 35 cents. In the next room, Jed coughed. Ruth froze as she heard her mother speak quietly to him. Bed springs squealed, followed by the protest of warped wooden boards as Francie went to the kitchen to fetch her husband some water. His coughing subsided. A second round of squealing springs announced Francie's return to bed.

Ruth waited an eternity, until Jed's coughing was replaced by a thready snore. She crept out of the house into a dark and silent street. Mahanoy was completely exhausted, as it was every night, until the company whistle blew the wake-up call at 5:30 in the morning.

She walked alone through the dark, praying not to encounter a coyote or stumble off the main road and break an ankle. Her coat was tight over the extra clothing, but she was warm. As the sun pushed weak light across a slag-colored sky, Ruth reached Delano, another mining town three miles north of Mahanoy.

The drugstore was open. Ruth bought a ticket to Hazelton, then slid onto a stool and spent a precious nickel on a cup of coffee and a biscuit. A single look at her filthy boots convinced her to sacrifice another nickel on a shoeshine to hide evidence of her nighttime walk.

As she waited for the bus, Ruth pretended that she was going to Hazleton to visit a sick cousin. If anyone asked, she'd toss her auburn braids and say airily that Sally Crosswater had the croup and needed nursing, but inside Ruth was terrified that Jed would send the mining company guards to drag her back to Mahanoy to face eternal damnation as a breaker. But no one approached.

When the Tonneau came, the driver punched her ticket and helped her step up into the back bench, next to a man from Delano who spat black saliva out the open side before folding his arms and sinking into himself. On the front bench, a wraith of a woman sat next to the driver and seemed similarly disinclined to chat.

"Here we go," the driver bellowed above the clattering of the motor.

The Tonneau shuddered, then belched sulfur as the wheels creaked forward. The canvas roof flapped and snapped like wet laundry in a stiff breeze. Delano went by in a moving panorama of scarred landscape and company houses. Ruth clutched her coin purse and braced herself as the machine rocked along the unpaved road.

She didn't look back.

January 1915

Astor Theatre, 1537 Broadway at 45th Street
New York City, New York

Ruth bowed with the rest of the cast as the final curtain came down on the Friday evening performance of *Hello, Broadway*, George M. Cohan's new musical review. She was the tall girl in the middle of the chorus line, the same position she'd occupied in half a dozen other Cohan & Harris productions.

"Nice work, girls." Mr. Cohan followed the chorus into the wings as the applause in the seats died away. As always, he went through the cast, thanking them for the performance before heading to his own dressing room.

He was Broadway's own firecracker. He wrote, directed, co-produced and starred in one hit musical show after another. Ruth admired him with every fiber of her being.

George M. Cohan was the lucky reason she hadn't starved to death when she first arrived in New York, still wearing layers of clothing and the remainder of Miss Prescott's money in her coin purse. Unintentionally interrupting a rehearsal for *Little Johnny Jones,* Ruth had walked into the Liberty Theatre simply because it was the first theater she saw. Mr. Cohan thought she was a replacement for one of the girls who'd left the show and hired her on the spot.

Little Johnny Jones had a massive cast. Ruth made friends and found a place to live with two other girls. When the show ended in New York, it went on the road. Ruth was in its second

Broadway iteration, too. After that, she owned the middle spot in *George Washington, Jr.* and *The Little Millionaire* and *The Man Who Owned Broadway* and *Broadway Jones* and *45 Minutes from Broadway*.

Every Cohan & Harris production was full of catchy tunes, comedic misunderstandings, and patriotic messages. Cohan's songs stuck in Ruth's head. They stuck in the theatergoing public's head, too, because almost every Cohan musical was a smash with over 100 performances. The sheet music for Cohan songs sold like hotcakes, too.

In between rehearsals and performances, Ruth went to other shows, ate in restaurants, bought herself fashionable clothes, and reveled in every new experience. Broadway was alive with excitement that blazed from the electric lights illuminating every theater marquee. Different colored lights burned out too fast, so every marquee was doused in white. The lights gave the theater district a catchy nickname: The Great White Way. The air there crackled with excitement and possibility.

Every time Ruth went to an audition, she was sure this was going to be her big chance at a speaking part. She read for small parts and big parts but somehow always ended up in the chorus line.

She wasn't lucky enough. Yet.

There was always a next time, or maybe the time after that. In the meantime, there was always another show, another party, another audition.

Dancing on Broadway and being associated with Cohan & Harris productions were tangible proof that dreams come true. She was so much more worldly than when she left Mahanoy.

Since then, she'd traveled in First Class train cars and dined in fine restaurants and lost her virginity. With Broadway shining all around and the footlights cheering her on, anything was possible.

The dressing room for the chorus was crowded with girls chattering like magpies and shedding sequined costumes. Ruth joined in, daubing cold cream on her face to take off greasepaint makeup. Street clothes, then a late supper with half a dozen friends from the cast. It was past midnight by the time she arrived at Lum's Ladies Boardinghouse, where she rented a closet-sized room by the week, a room that was all hers for the first time in her life.

Ruth unpinned her hat, hung up her coat, and saw that Mrs. Lum had left mail on the pillow. The envelope decorated with Miss Prescott's familiar cursive was a lovely treat. Years ago, Ruth paid back those fateful five dollars, with interest. The two women stayed in touch. Ruth always sent gifts for Christmas and her teacher's birthday. Miss Prescott even came to New York a few years ago when Ruth was in *George Washington, Jr*.

Yawning as she nestled under the quilt in her flannel nightgown, Ruth opened the envelope and drew out a letter and a small newspaper clipping.

Dear Ruthie, I'm sorry to have to give you much bad news. To begin, your mother passed from the pleurisy and was buried a week ago last Saturday . . .

Ruth put down the letter and studied the clipping. It was her mother's obituary from the mining company's broadsheet dated January 5, 1915:

Mrs. Francie Hogan of Number 17, Miner's Row,

Mahanoy, died at home, age 45. Reverend John Munter praised her as a hard worker and a good mother to her three boys. Mrs. Hogan's husband Jed passed four years ago. Mrs. Hogan was a member of the Homemaker's Society and attended the Miner's Chapel every Sunday.

There was no mention of Ruthie June Crosswater or of Ruth's father, Bill Crosswater. Ruth knew she should not be surprised or hurt by the omission, but she was.

When Ruth left Mahanoy, Francie struck her daughter out of her life. Ruth wrote to Francie many times but never received a reply, although the money she sent never came back. She even asked Miss Prescott to deliver a letter in person. Francie never answered that one, either. That's when Ruth stopped sending money.

She blamed Jed. No doubt he'd given Francie a choice between him and her rebellious daughter and Francie chose him.

Miss Prescott was Ruth's last link to her mother, keeping her abreast of details about Francie's life in Mahanoy, not that much ever changed. Jed's boys grew old enough to work the breakers and then to go down in the pit themselves. When Jed died of the black lung, Francie stayed and kept house for the boys.

Ruth set the clipping aside and read more bad news.

Miss Prescott had a cancer that would take her in a year or so, the doctor said. She was preparing to move into a home for old teachers in Hazleton.

She loved Ruthie and was so proud of her. That five dollars was the best money she ever spent.

Miss Prescott's diagnosis hit Ruth harder than her own

mother's passing. After a good cry, Ruth decided that when *Hello Broadway* ended, she'd go to Hazleton. Take care of Miss Prescott until the end.

There would always be another show, another chance to make it big on Broadway.

August 1922

Star Hotel for Women
Albany, New York

"I can't believe it's our last night together," Ruth said. She hugged her knees as a pang of remorse tugged at her heart. Under the lumpy mattress, the ancient bedsprings squealed a rusty protest.

"We've been the four Varsity Sisters forever," Vivian wailed from the opposite bed. She was the baby of the group, with a pink pout and a puff of bleached hair. "It won't be the same."

"Don't make Ruthie feel bad." Sitting cross-legged next to Vivian, Cora lit a cigarette with the silver lighter that some stage-door Johnny had given her last year. In between puffs, she tossed a fringe of black bangs out of her eyes and exhaled out the window.

In exchange for the tobacco smoke drifting away from the Star Hotel for Women, the city of Albany offered the sounds of a humid summer night. The air was heavy with a thunderstorm that refused to show itself. Murmurs of lovers, window-shopping the stores which had closed hours ago, drifted up to their room on the third floor along with shouts from tired pushcart vendors selling lemonade and fizzy tonics. The chatter of those who'd been to the cinema to see the evening showing of *Blood and Sand* with Rudolph Valentino and Nita Naldi was better than any critic's review.

Automobiles and omnibuses rumbled past the hotel. The

flickering neon sign on the side of the building sent momentary oblongs of yellow across the walls of the hotel room and teased the well-worn trunks and valises waiting for the next city, the next theater, the next show.

"You'll find someone to replace me," Ruth said. She took a few dozen bobby pins and began pinning her daringly short auburn hair into curls. In the morning, she'd have a head of bouncy waves.

"Of course, we won't," Vivian said and accepted Cora's offer of a drag on the cigarette.

Ruth scooted over as Lurlene, clad in cotton summer pajamas like the other three women, climbed aboard. The springs groaned as the bed swayed.

"Don't cry, Viv." Lurlene reached across the space between the two beds and took the cigarette from Vivian. "This is Ruthie's last night. Party time. No crying." She took a deep drag and waved smoke out the window.

The last pin-curl in place, Ruth smiled at Vivian. "It was bound to happen sometime, honey. I thought you'd be the first to go."

"I thought it would be me, too." Vivian sniffed and laughed at the same time. The maudlin mood, which had been threatening to sour the evening, dissipated.

Cora produced a battered metal flask. "Ruthie gets the first slug."

"What is it?"

"He said it was genuine Irish whiskey," Cora said. "Cost three dollars, too."

"Three dollars." Lurlene grinned. "Sounds like the good kind."

Ruth unscrewed the cap and sniffed. Her eyes watered. "Lordy."

She swallowed a healthy mouthful, and the whiskey burned its way down her gullet. It was the real stuff, not the bathtub gin that was becoming popular as Prohibition agents destroyed stocks of beer and liquor. When she could breathe again, they all burst out laughing. Ruth passed the flask to Lurlene, who could drink lye without flinching.

The flask went around another time and Ruth felt herself getting teary. She'd never get another chance like she had now, but leaving the act was taking all her courage.

Ruthie, Lurlene, Vivian, Cora. They'd spent five years on the vaudeville circuit together, playing second-tier theaters up and down the east coast from Montreal to Tampa. The Varsity Sisters was a song and dance act with a collegiate theme, although the closest any of them had ever come to higher education was the night Cora spent in the back seat of a Princeton boy's flivver. From theater to hotel to train station, the four women had performed together, eaten together, and gossiped together. When the money ran short, they even shared beds together in cramped hotel rooms like this one.

A few men came and went, and Ruth fell in love a few times, but she never could imagine making a home with any of them, even if that home was a hotel on the road.

Ruth was the unspoken leader who managed their bookings and fought to get the act's name printed in bigger letters on theater playbills. The other three looked up to her, not just because she was older, but because Ruth had been on Broadway with George M. Cohan in *Little Johnny Jones* and all those other Cohan & Harris shows.

She came back to New York after Miss Prescott died, but Broadway had moved on without her. Ruth wasn't chosen for any of the big name shows and found herself dancing in second-tier theaters. "Off-Broadway" they called it. The other dancers were younger, chasing the bigger shows, the bigger marquees.

When even Off-Broadway producers began to bypass Ruth in favor of younger girls, she kicked up her heels in whatever vaudeville act would take her. Lurlene was in the same predicament when they met behind a theater in Portland, Maine, smoking their respective last gaspers and shivering like idiots with their suitcases as they waited for the stage manager to open up.

They combined Lurlene's voice and Ruth's legs into the first Varsity Sisters act. Those legs held an audience's attention, despite the fact that she was on the far side of thirty and her Broadway credentials no longer provided entrée to the best chorus lines. The notion of home became an abstract yearning for something she never had.

And then William came along.

"Three Varsity Sisters is enough." Lurlene bumped Ruth's shoulder with her own. "Three is a lucky number. We don't need to replace Ruthie. I mean, it's not like we could, anyway."

"Ruthie, we got you a present." Vivian bounced off the bed, opened a trunk, and pulled out a large box wrapped in shiny white paper. She handed it to Ruth. "It's from all of us."

Ruth prised away the paper to see a box bearing the logo of Churchwell's department store. "Churchwell's," she marveled. It was the nicest store in Albany.

"Go on, open it," Lurlene urged her.

"Whatever's inside, it's too expensive." Ruth was almost afraid to open the box.

Cora rolled her eyes. "How many times does a gal meet the man of her dreams?"

"About eight," Vivian said solemnly, prompting more whiskey-fueled laughter.

Ruth set aside the lid, parted the tissue paper, and found a mint green silk peignoir set edged with ecru lace. A dozen silk-covered buttons lingered down the front of the fitted robe while thin shoulder straps ensured that the nightgown left little to the imagination.

"It's beautiful," Ruth said, stunned at the richness of the going-away gift. "Too beautiful to wear."

"It's for your wedding night," Vivian said. "It'll look fantastic with your hair."

"Do you think William will love it?" Cora asked.

"Of course he'll love it," Lurlene said shortly.

Ruth had a few farewell gifts for her friends as well. Silk stockings for Vivian, a cigarette case for Cora, a monogrammed notebook for Lurlene. The four women stayed up until their eyelids were gritty, sharing cigarettes, whiskey, and rose-colored memories of vaudeville.

Tomorrow morning, the three remaining Varsity Sisters would take the train north to Plattsburgh, the next stop on the current tour. Ruth and William would head to Boston and their future together.

William was an acrobat on the vaudeville circuit, although he was an excellent hoofer, too. Compact and lithe, he had a shock of blonde hair, a quick wit, boundless energy, and eyes that sparked blue fire. The first time they met, just three months ago, he'd walked on his hands to impress her. When he proposed both marriage and a ballroom dance act, Ruth nearly died of happiness. She'd waited her whole life to fall in love this hard.

With Ruth's legs and William's impresario contacts, the world was their oyster. William had a friend who knew a guy who knew someone in Boston casting a new show for the top-tier Pantages circuit. They would audition in just two days.

"Ballroom Expressions with William and June Wilson" was an athletic combination of ballroom quickstep and William's handstands and backflips. Audiences had seen an acrobat in a jester costume, but an acrobat in a tuxedo with a beautiful, leggy partner would be a bigger success than the famous ballroom dance duo of Vernon and Irene Castle.

William wrote advertising copy for the Pantages circuit to promote the act and decided that Ruth would now go by her middle name and pretend she was from Philadelphia. "June" was swell and sophisticated, William insisted. "Ruth" was old-fashioned. "Ruthie" was even worse.

Goodbye, Ruthie June Crosswater. Hello, June Wilson.

Ruth fingered the mint green silk. June Wilson. Mrs. William Wilson. William promised that they would get married as soon as their big break delivered enough money for a proper wedding. Ruth deserved the best, he insisted, not some hasty justice of the peace ceremony. In the meantime, William would sign hotel registers as Mr. and Mrs. William Wilson so they wouldn't be arrested for indecency.

Outside the window, the city of Albany quieted. Vivian fell asleep, her back plastered against the wall. Cora finished the whiskey and started to snore. Ruth turned out the light.

Next to her, Lurlene's breathing grew soft and even.

Ruth was exhausted from dancing two shows, hauling her trunk to the hotel, and staying up so late. But sleep was elusive. She thought of William at the Graves Hotel with the other men in the troupe. Tomorrow night they'd be in Boston, lying in each other's arms as Mr. and Mrs. Wilson.

"Ruthie?" Lurlene whispered. "Are you awake?"

Ruth wriggled onto her side to face Lurlene. "Can't you sleep?"

"I'll miss you, Ruthie."

"I'll miss you, too."

Lurlene's eyes glittered in the dark as they searched Ruth's face. "Are you sure about William?"

Maybe it was the whiskey or the late hour or the delayed marriage, but for a moment Ruth had no reply. "Of course, I'm sure," she finally managed. "Why would you say that?"

"I just . . . I don't know. It all happened so fast." Lurlene hesitated. "William is so handsome, but he's pushy, too. I want to make sure you're happy."

"He's not pushy," Ruth said. "He just wants the best for us. You should be happy for me."

"I am." Lurlene's teeth were a flash of white as she gave Ruth a watery smile.

Fighting a lump in her throat, Ruth turned so that her back was to Lurlene. The protesting bedsprings surrendered to the first distant boom of thunder.

November 1922

The Temple Theatre, 35 Clinton Street
Rochester, New York

"You're moving like a sack of potatoes," William said. He abruptly released Ruth from the ballroom hold, making no effort to hide his irritation. "What's the matter with you?"

"I'm just tired," Ruth lied. "I'll be fine tonight."

"Are you done rehearsing?" the pianist called from the otherwise empty orchestra pit.

"Apparently." William stalked across the stage, reached over the footlights, and paid the pianist.

The tiers of red velvet upholstered seats were empty, as were the box seats in the balconies. The only people in the theater that afternoon to witness William's rude behavior were the usual mix of managers and cleaners getting ready for the evening show, but Ruth was still embarrassed.

She looked around. In the wings on either side of the stage, the backstage crew was busy, adjusting the ropes and pulleys that raised and lowered the curtains, scrims, and backdrops. Mr. Diller, the troupe manager, was there, too, organizing props for the magic act. He didn't meet Ruth's eye.

William trotted down the stage steps and shrugged on the tweed coat he'd left draped across the front row.

"Where are you going?" Ruth asked.

"Go back to the hotel and take a nap," William said brusquely. "I need to send a telegram. Make sure Murphy in New York is waiting for us."

"All right." Ruth was too tired to do anything else.

With unexpected gentleness, William kissed her on the cheek before striding up the side aisle to the front door of the theater. Ruth forced herself into her own coat and trudged through the snow to the hotel.

She didn't need a doctor to tell her that she was pregnant. Three, maybe four months along. If William suspected, he didn't let on. She never undressed in front of him. Fashionably loose dresses hid her thickening waist.

Her timing was terrible. Their big break had yet to materialize, and money was tight. Meanwhile, William spent too much on restaurants and First Class train seats.

They'd pinned their hopes on the Boston impresario casting for the Pantages circuit but he scorned the combination of acrobatics and ballroom dancing of "Ballroom Expressions with William and June Wilson" and didn't sign them. In a knee-jerk reaction to the flinty rejection, William signed a contract with Mr. Diller's vaudeville troupe playing small and medium-sized cities in Ohio, Indiana, and western New York. "Ballroom Expressions with William and June Wilson" got bottom billing.

Diller's vaudeville troupe was the usual mix of song-and-dance acts, with a dog show and magician thrown in for good measure. The whole thing was fairly campy, meaning that audiences were primed for hoots and laughter when William stopped dancing and began his tumbling routine. Once again, Ruth suggested that they forget the cartwheels and handstands in favor of a straight ballroom performance like Vernon and Irene Castle, but William refused.

They still weren't married. Although he continued to sign

hotel registers as Mr. and Mrs. William Wilson, William insisted they wait. Their wedding would be done right, he kept saying.

Ruth dreaded telling him that she was pregnant. His temper had been hot lately, and tonight was their last show. Mr. Diller's troupe would go on to Syracuse, but William was determined to take their act to Broadway. No more small cities where people didn't understand what he was trying to do.

She lumbered through the evening performance. William twisted himself inside out for the audience, but the applause was desultory. Later, as they lay in bed in the hotel, Ruth almost told him about the baby, but she fell asleep before the words came out of her mouth.

"I need cigarettes," William said the next morning as they breakfasted on toast and coffee in the hotel dining room. "I'll run over to the tobacco shop while you finish packing your suitcase. We've got plenty of time before the train."

Ruth nodded. "All right."

He flashed the blue-eyed smile she couldn't resist. "Broadway is going to be our big break. I just know it."

"William, I have something to tell you," Ruth blurted as he stood up.

William tossed his napkin on the table. "What?"

As quickly as it came, Ruth's courage deserted her. "I love you," she said lamely. "I know you're right about Broadway."

"I love you, too." William made a show of looking around at the other diners, intent on their coffee and newspapers, then bent and kissed her. "You're my everything, June. Always and forever."

Back upstairs, William put on his coat and hat, hefted his

suitcase with one hand and patted his coat pocket with the other. "I've got our tickets right here. Do you need anything while I'm at the shop?"

Milk and baby clothes and a doctor. Ruth shook her head. "No, thank you." She pointed to his suitcase. "Leave it. The bellhop can take it when he gets mine."

"I don't mind," William said. "Wait for me in the lobby."

He kissed her and walked out of the room.

Ruth took her time packing, then gave the bellhop a nickel to carry her suitcase downstairs and turn in her room key. William wasn't back from his errand yet so she sat in the little parlor to wait. Outside the window, white snow swirled against Rochester's red bricks. Pedestrians rushed by with heads bent against the cold, scarves covering mouths and noses, buckles on galoshes jingling.

After 30 minutes, Ruth went to the front desk. "Have you seen my husband?" she asked the clerk. "William Wilson."

"Not since he left earlier." The clerk was a young man with owlish spectacles and brilliantined hair wearing an intimidating uniform doused with gold braid.

"Yes, of course," Ruth said uneasily. "We're going to New York today." Where had William gone?

The clerk flipped through a neat stack of cards. "That will be eleven dollars, Mrs. Wilson."

"Eleven dollars?"

"Two nights and breakfast both mornings." The clerk waited expectantly.

"Mr. Wilson was supposed to pay the bill," Ruth said. William managed their finances, including paying for hotel rooms, restaurants, and train tickets. She barely had fifteen dollars in her purse and there wouldn't be any more until they signed a new contract.

"It's past check out time," the clerk said meaningfully.

"Of course." Ruth's cheeks were warm as she carefully counted out the right amount. Had William forgotten? Had something happened to him?

She waited another 30 minutes in the parlor, conscious of the clerk's eye, her sense of unease growing although there was still plenty of time before the train to New York City.

The bellhop approached. "Mr. Bedford at the front would like to know if we can find you a taxi, ma'am."

"No. I . . . I'll walk."

Ruth asked to store her suitcase, drew on her gloves and galoshes and headed into the falling snow. Her first stop was the tobacco shop around the corner. No one answering William's description had been in that morning.

Sick with worry, Ruth wrapped her scarf tighter and hurried to the theater. The stage door was unlocked, giving her a reprieve from the scudding wind and slick sidewalks. She darted inside and found the theater manager in his messy cubbyhole of an office looking through receipts.

"Has William Wilson been here this morning?" Ruth asked.

"The acrobat fella? No, no one's been here besides the stagehands."

"What about Mr. Diller?" she pressed. "The troupe manager. Has he been here?"

"I thought you bunch was on the way to Syracuse."

The temperature dropped as the snow thickened. Ruth battled her way to the train station, her rounding stomach as heavy as lead. Her brain raced with possible reasons William might have needed to speak with Mr. Diller that he hadn't thought to share with her. Perhaps a last-minute business chat. She pushed herself through the crowds to find the list of departing trains. The express to Syracuse left in twelve minutes.

By the time Ruth found Mr. Diller, she was out of breath, her nose was dripping from the cold, and she had a stitch in her side. The manager was huddled inside his big black overcoat, a homburg hat jammed low over his ears, as he rounded up performers and got them aboard the train.

"Mr. Diller!" Ruth managed, her lungs heaving.

"June?" Mr. Diller was clearly surprised to see her.

"Have you seen William today?" Ruth asked.

Mr. Diller moved apart from the group, motioning Ruth to follow. "Weren't you going to New York?"

"Yes." Ruth grabbed his coat sleeve. "Have you seen William today?"

"I saw him an hour ago. Running hell-bent for leather with his suitcase. Jumped on a train as it was pulling out. Had a dame with him, keeping up as fast as you please." Mr. Diller trailed off as the situation dawned on him. "I thought that was you."

"You must be mistaken," Ruth heard herself say. "That couldn't have been William."

Mr. Diller shook his head. "Same tweed coat, same hat as when I paid him off last night. He take your share?"

The train whistle blew, a great gout of steam billowed over the track, and the conductor shouted. Last-minute passengers swarmed toward the train, even as they called final farewells over their shoulders. Porters pushed hand trucks laden with suitcases, wheels groaning against the concrete platform. The conductor shouted a warning. Carriage doors slammed.

"I've got to go, June," Mr. Diller said over the din. "Face it. Wilson's a scoundrel. You're better off without him."

Ruth trudged back to the hotel. The snow lashed down harder, with a wind that cut through her cloth coat.

She waited in the parlor all day, numb with disbelief, until the snooty desk clerk asked if she wanted to check in again. The parlor was for paying guests only.

Ruth collected her suitcase and left. The five dollars in her purse was all the money she had in the world. She had no idea what to do next.

February 1923

Third Class, New York Central Railroad

Ruth fell asleep as the train clattered its way to Poughkeepsie.

She was exhausted from dragging herself from place to place looking for a job and sleeping in cheap hotels that catered to vaudeville performers. As the weeks turned into months, Ruth ran out of energy, money, and tears. She sold the lingerie from Churchwell's and her best pair of shoes to keep going. Although most of the time she was turned away for being pregnant and single, theater managers who remembered her from the Varsity Sisters gave her odd jobs. Coat check girl in Seneca Falls for a week when the regular girl was ill. Costume assistant for a show passing through Ithaca. She cleaned the toilets in a theater in Cortland but left when the head janitor pushed her against the wall for a kiss.

After the new year, she ended up in Albany working in a commercial laundry. The work was exhausting. One of the laundry's clients was Miss Culver, who ran the Star Hotel for Women. She knew of a position in a theater near Vassar College in Poughkeepsie, and was kind enough to wire ahead to say that Ruth was coming to apply. She wasn't kind enough, however, to let an unwed pregnant woman stay in her hotel.

The pregnancy sapped Ruth, although the baby had stopped moving so much. For the past week she'd leaked blood. All of her nice Munsingwear slips were stained, as were several of her dresses. There was nothing to be done except push on, get a job, and hope for the best.

Ruth snapped awake when the conductor came through the aisles, shouting that Poughkeepsie was the next stop. Getting to her feet provoked a wave of dizziness and she swayed uncertainly as she reached for her suitcase in the overhead rack. Some man pulled it down for her.

"Are you all right?" The man's voice sounded strange, as if he was speaking in a tunnel.

"I'm fine." Ruth took a deep breath, closed her hand around the handle of the suitcase, and forced herself to stay standing as the train slowed.

Pain sliced through her side as Ruth left the train station. She nearly dropped her suitcase as she passed through the big station doors. Her whole body contracted. Bent over and dizzy, she waited for the sensation to abate as people rushed by. When she could finally take a breath, Ruth saw a small park ahead. It was a slushy palette of brown grass and melting white snow with a couple of wooden benches.

Ruth made it to a bench before another wave of pain shook her body. She sucked in air before it happened again. The next wave came with a gush of hot wetness between her thighs. She pulled the hem of her coat aside to see bright red blood trickling down her leg, soaking her silk stockings and taffeta slip.

Her body was wracked again and Ruth realized she was having the baby, right there on a park bench. She looked around for help, but there was no one around. Before she could think of what to do, a long spasm convulsed every muscle.

Her chest froze. Ruth couldn't breathe. The pain was everywhere and everything; the present, past and future. Ruth's teeth chattered and her hands shook as the flow of blood turned into a river and then her body pushed out a horrible dark pulpy mess.

The dull colors of the park spun around her, faster and faster until everything disappeared in a sucking whirlpool of pain.

February 1923

Duchess County Hospital
Poughkeepsie, New York

Ruth blinked.

A man's face swam into view, nose webbed with red veins. "Are you Ruthie June Crosswater?" He rattled a piece of paper at her. "This birth certificate was in your suitcase."

He had on a uniform. A policeman's blue uniform.

Ruth wanted to ask him for help, but she was shivering uncontrollably. Her mouth was full of chattering teeth.

"Ruthie June Crosswater, you're under arrest," he said. "Lewd behavior, indecent exposure, and the rest. We don't hold with that kind of behavior here in Poughkeepsie, missy."

There was a commotion and the policeman was confronted by a man in a white smock. "You can arrest her if she survives the night," the man snapped. "Right now, she's hemorrhaging to death."

A different face with a toothbrush mustache hovered over Ruth. "I'm Doctor Morris," he said. "Your condition is very grave. We have to operate to stop the bleeding."

Ruth was dimly aware of others circling around as she swam through the rich, warm pain. Their voices were loud and strident, blending together in a frenetic pulse she didn't understand. An evil-smelling cloth pressed over her nose and mouth and the world slid away.

The next time she woke, sunlight streamed through pale muslin curtains. Ruth was in a bed with stiffly starched sheets.

Her entire body ached. She was thirsty beyond belief.

A nurse in a long white dress and a frilled cap sat next to the bed, leafing through a copy of *Motion Picture* magazine. Between Ruth's bed and the nurse's chair, a small wooden nightstand held an enamel tray laden with a pitcher of water and a glass.

"Water," Ruth croaked. "Can I have some water?"

"Oh my." The nurse bolted to her feet, hastily popped the magazine into the nightstand drawer and darted through an opening in the curtain. She reappeared a moment later followed by the man with the toothbrush mustache and white smock.

"I'm Dr. Morris," he said. "We met before, but you might not remember."

"I'm very thirsty," Ruth whispered.

Dr. Morris nodded to the nurse, and she gave Ruth a sip of water.

"Do you recall what happened to you, Mrs. Crosswater?" he asked after she swallowed.

"Something went wrong with the baby. In the park."

"The child did not develop normally and had been dead for some time." The doctor spoke in a straightforward manner. "You're lucky to be alive. Were you under a doctor's care?"

"No."

"Where is your husband? He should be notified."

Ruth gave her head a tiny shake. "He's gone."

"Gone where?"

"I don't know."

"Ah. I see." Dr. Morris seemed to thaw a fraction. "You had a suitcase. Here to visit family?"

Ruth blinked back tears. "I was here for a job. All the way

from Albany."

Dr. Morris raised his eyebrows in an expression that combined both surprise and discomfort. "Well, you won't be going anywhere for quite some time. Your condition is precarious, at best. You suffered severe blood loss and a complete hysterectomy was necessary to stop the bleeding. You'll experience more in the next few weeks and we'll watch for sepsis."

"A complete hysterectomy?" Ruth didn't know what that meant.

"The nurse will explain," Dr. Morris said shortly. "A woman your age has no business getting pregnant. Of course, you're sterile now. No doubt for the best."

Two policemen came the next day, announced the charges against her, and threatened to handcuff Ruth to the iron bed frame if she tried to leave the hospital.

Miss Redding was the nurse who attended to Ruth during the day. She brought beef broth, tea, applesauce, and cheery gossip about Betty Compson and Marion Mack, two of the nurse's favorite film stars. The night nurse glided in when the lights were out. Time passed in a blur of sponge baths, changes of her soiled bandages, and helpless bouts of tears.

Dr. Morris came in the mornings to check her stitches and give instructions to the nurses. Policemen dropped in every few days to remind Ruth that she was under arrest.

It was two weeks before the doctor even let Ruth get out of the bed. When she did, she was as weak as a kitten. Ruth saw that she was in a ward of six beds, each curtained off for privacy. By the time Miss Redding helped her to shuffle to the window at the end of the ward, Ruth was out of breath.

The bleeding eventually petered out and Ruth's strength slowly returned. It felt like a huge accomplishment when she managed to walk down the aisle between the beds all by herself. Soon she shuffled up and down dozens of times a day, bored to tears, and torn between abject humiliation and desperation. She thought constantly of asking Miss Redding to write a letter to Lurlene but couldn't think of what to say or how to say it.

Humiliation won. Ruth didn't contact anyone.

It was after one of her pacing sessions that Ruth sat in the nurse's chair and opened a drawer in the nightstand, hoping to find something to read. Miss Redding's latest movie magazine would do nicely.

There was no magazine, however, just a pile of the *Poughkeepsie Eagle-News*. Ruth happily spread them out on the bed, only to find that she was a front-page sensation known as *Park Mother*. Headline after headline trumpeted Ruth's sins:

Park Mother Delivers Malformed Baby in Public

Vassar College Shields Students from Park Mother's Indecency

Mayor Delivers Moral Message After Park Mother Outcry

Judge Vows Park Mother's Indecency Will be Punished

Hospital Cites Critical Condition, Prevents Journalists from Questioning Park Mother

Ruth read every article, eyes brimming with tears of shame and embarrassment. The newspapers didn't call her by name but shamed her as a woman of loose morals. They didn't know about "Ballroom Expressions with William and June Wilson" or how he'd left her high and dry with barely five dollars in her purse and a baby on the way. In fact, none of the articles even mentioned the requirement of male participation when it came to *Park Mother's* indecent condition.

The guilt was hers alone. Ruth was soiled, tarnished, a compromised woman forever.

Hollow, too. The doctor saved her life, but all the internal plumbing that made her a child-bearing woman was gone.

She stayed in the hospital for six weeks, slowly gathering her strength. When the day came for her to be released, two policemen collected Ruth and her suitcase, bundled her into a car, and took her to the Duchess County courthouse where she was formally charged with vagrancy, lewd behavior, indecent exposure, and public indecency. The same afternoon she stood before a judge and admitted to being guilty of all charges. After a long-winded diatribe on his duty to punish declining morals, the judge sentenced her to six months behind bars, after which she would not be welcome in Poughkeepsie again.

The gavel cracked, the bailiff hoisted an unresisting Ruth by one arm, and she was led out of the courtroom.

PART 2: LUCA

September 1906

Near the village of Serra San Bruno
Calabria, Italy

Gianluca Lombardo would always remember the day the soldiers rode their horses into the olive grove looking for his father.

He was five years old and helping to fill the vented metal buckets, collecting the olives off the muslin cloth puddled at the base of the trees as his father Matteo shook the branches and they played the counting game.

"I have 93 olives, Luca," Matteo said. "Take away 37. Now how many do I have?"

"Easy, Papa. Fifty-six."

"All right. If you have 56, how many more to make 923?"

Unlike his swarthy Calabrian relatives, Luca was fair like Matteo, with hazel eyes and a mop of light brown hair. He dropped more olives in the bucket, keeping track of the number even as another part of his brain answered his father's question. "Eight hundred and sixty-seven."

The game was a secret language that Luca and his father Matteo shared. They counted olives and stones and bricks in the church wall and the number of people in the village square. Luca's mother Viola listened and smiled, but it wasn't her game. She was happiest in the evenings when the little family of three was alone in their snug stone house and her handsome husband Matteo read aloud. His small collection of well-thumbed books took them to new places, Viola always said.

The three of them, soaring from their nest like birds in the sky, all because Matteo could read.

Luca could read, too. His father constantly taught him new words.

His grandfather's olive grove greedily absorbed the sun as Luca's extended family gathered the harvest. Theirs was a happy family, and the work was accompanied by shouts and laughter and scolding as Luca's younger cousins paid no attention to their mother.

The grove was ringed by three houses. The paths between them were well-worn.

The largest house belonged to Faustino and Domenica Russo, Luca's grandparents. Viola was their eldest daughter, the rebellious one who married a stranger. Matteo Lombardo wasn't from Serra San Bruno. He wasn't even from Calabria where the people were known for *la testa dura*, that is to say, being exceptionally hard-headed.

Matteo Lombardo was from the Lombardy region in the far north of Italy. No one quite knew how this educated man came to be so far from home in Serra San Bruno, but he was a good worker and when he married Viola, her father built the second house. The third house belonged to Viola's brother Arturo Russo, his always-pregnant wife and their brood of children.

The counting game paused as Matteo went to help his brother-in-law. By far the tallest person there, Matteo was always the one who gently shook the branches or prodded the treetops with a stick to release the olives. Luca worked alongside his cousin Enzo, who was five years older. Enzo didn't play the counting game, but he was strong and sturdy and Luca's best friend.

Matteo taught Enzo to read, too.

The ground shook with the sound of rolling thunder as horses approached. Soldiers galloped through the olive grove, ripping leaves and twigs off the centuries-old trees and shouting as they descended upon the stunned family. Luca was awestruck at the ornate uniforms and tall brimmed caps.

Enzo yanked him out of the way as one of the soldiers hurtled past, an officer with a sword in his hand and a red patch with gold stars on his uniform. Foam flew from his horse's mouth. A wave of animal heat washed over the two boys as the beast kicked over the bucket of olives. Two hundred and sixteen olives spilled onto the ground and were mashed by the enormous hooves.

His grandmother and aunt screamed as the soldiers circled the grove, sending up choking clouds of dust. A 15 foot phalanx of soldiers followed the horses, long rifles pointed menacingly.

"What do you want?" Luca's grandfather shouted. "We are peasants. We have nothing."

"*Primo Capitano* Matteo Lombardo!" The officer reined in his horse in front of Luca's father. The beast juddered to a snorting stop, flanks heaving, bridle jangling.

"I am Matteo Lombardo," Luca's father said quietly, squinting up at the officer.

"*Primo Capitano* Matteo Lombardo, you are wanted for desertion from the Army of King Victor Emmanuel."

Luca's father said nothing, but his gaze went first to Luca, then to Viola.

"Do you understand?" the officer barked. He had a

luxurious mustache and a white scar that curved like a scimitar around the side of his chin. "The charge is desertion. You must come with us."

The foot soldiers clustered around Matteo and tied his hands behind his back.

"No!" Viola launched herself at them, clawing to get to her husband. They threw her off.

"Wait for me," Matteo called over his shoulder to her as they marched him away. "Take care of Luca until I get back."

"You have harbored a fugitive," the officer shouted at the family as he wheeled his horse around, further trampling the harvest. The scar stood out brightly against the shadow of his beard. "A deserter. Your land is hereby forfeit to the decision of a military tribunal."

He spurred his horse and galloped away.

No one moved until the sound of boots and hooves faded away. Then Viola gave a wrenching sob and fell to the ground, weeping uncontrollably.

Luca twisted out of Enzo's grasp and ran to his mother.

Distant shots tore through the air and hovered in the still blue sky.

Viola leaped to her feet. "No!"

She took off running, Luca at her heels. But she was faster in her rope-soled shoes and husband's trousers and quickly outdistanced her son. Her long dark hair escaped from its kerchief and streamed down her back as she flew over the uneven ground toward the fading echo of gunfire.

Matteo's lifeless body was tied to a scrubby pine in an unplowed field east of the olive grove. His hair glinted like brass in the bright sunshine. His chin sagged against his bloody chest.

A firing squad of five men was on the ground a little distance away, collars loosened, still cleaning their rifles as the other soldiers watched. The officers had dismounted and were feasting on bread and salami, washed down with bottles of red wine.

Viola threw herself against her husband's body. "Matteo, no, no!"

"The punishment for desertion is execution." The officer with the scar swung onto his horse and cantered toward Viola as she sobbed. "He was a deserter, and he was punished."

"You bastard!" Viola raged, tears streaming down her face. She spat on the ground in front of him. "You are a coward to kill a good man. I curse you for a coward! A coward--"

The officer raised his revolver and shot Viola with no more emotion than if he was lifting a fork to his mouth. She fell dead at Matteo's feet.

Luca stopped at the edge of the olive grove and his brain took refuge in the counting game. The officer's gun was identical to the revolver that his father kept under the bed which held six bullets. Four officers meant 24 bullets. Plus each of the fifteen soldiers must have six bullets, too. Subtract five for his father and one for his mother and the group had 108 bullets left.

The officers rounded up their troops. The soldiers disappeared over the hill, leaving the two bodies where they lay. No one noticed the little boy standing in the shelter of the olive grove.

June 1918

Rectory of Our Lady of Sorrows Catholic Church
Serra San Bruno, Calabria, Italy

No one had ever asked Luca if he wanted to be a priest, yet the plan for the 17-year-old to enter the seminary was beyond question for everyone except himself and Rafaella Benedetto.

But Rafaella was just an illiterate girl, the daughter of an illiterate farmer. Luca's fate was hardly up to her.

Luca knew that he had few options. As the son of a criminal, he would not inherit his grandfather's olive grove. The land that sustained the family would pass to his uncle, Enzo's father. The uncle in turn made it clear that when Luca reached adulthood, the meager gifts of the dry Calabrian dirt would no longer be shared with Matteo Lombardo's son.

His cousin Enzo left for America three years ago. Luca fought tears but the rest of the family heaved a visible sigh of relief. Enzo's passage across the Atlantic cost the family dearly but was an investment in survival. When he got himself established in America, Enzo would send money to sustain those left behind. Again, Luca's uncle made it known that the son of Matteo Lombardo would not share in Enzo's largesse.

For his grandparents and uncle, Luca was the embodiment of his mother's disastrous choice of husband. Viola's son looked too much like his father. Luca wasn't quite as tall or as fair, but as he grew, Matteo's hazel eyes, chestnut hair, quiet demeanor and love of learning became more and more pronounced. Yet his Calabrian mother had passed on quick fists, a muscular frame, and daydreams of somewhere else, all things Luca needed more than most.

Cruel gossip about the deserter from the north and the local girl who fell under his spell still swirled through the village of Serra San Bruno. Luca was more or less an outcast, but respected by his enemies. He never started a fight, but he never lost one, either.

There were still chores to be done, even for a future priest. Luca worked the fields for his grandfather, went to school when he could, and was tutored by Father Caviglia in the evenings. As long as the priest didn't expect to be paid, Luca's grandfather tolerated the lessons.

On a good day, Luca might see Rafaella. Her family's farm wasn't far from the church and they could have a minute to themselves in the dark on the edge of the village before he walked back to his grandparents' house.

As the weeks went by, the examinations Luca would take to secure his place in the seminary took on the cast of an executioner's axe. Every time he saw Rafaella, his heart ached for what he would leave behind. Whenever they found a moment alone in the dark, their hands explored each other with increasing desperation.

Father Caviglia lectured Luca innumerable times on a priest's vow of celibacy and the requirement to remain pure, but all those words slid away when Luca was with Rafaella. She wasn't the prettiest girl in the village, but she was slender and kind, with clever eyes and a crooked smile that her mother lamented was the sign of the devil but Luca thought was perfect.

Rafaella gave herself to him in the hayloft of her father's barn a few months before the examinations. For ten terrifying and utterly silent minutes, they fumbled together in the straw, desire overcoming the fear of being discovered. Rafaella's brothers would be ruthless if they knew the village outcast had defiled their only sister.

Three weeks later, opportunity beckoned a second time. They came together in the hayloft again for another few minutes of thrilling awkwardness in the pitch dark while the goats bleated below them. Rafaella breathed into Luca's ear that she loved him, that she never wanted him to leave her.

The days marched inexorably toward the date of his examinations, punctuated by stolen moments and forbidden intimacy. And a beast called Latin, the language of the Church.

The examination was only ten days away on the night Luca began translating Tacitus's *Annals of Imperial Rome*. Father Caviglia gave Luca a fresh sheet of paper and carefully turned the page in the Latin text. "Do the third book."

Latin was the most challenging subject Luca had to master, but tonight he'd done well. His translation of *Liber I* and *Liber II* was faultless. He still got a lecture, of course. Father Caviglia constantly hectored Luca on mental discipline as well as his Latin skills. The ancient priest was a hard taskmaster, swaddled in his equally ancient cassock despite the heat that persisted into the evening, yet he always gave Luca something to eat and a glass of wine.

If the examination was only mathematics and history, Luca would not have to study at all. In school, he sucked up information like a sponge, answering questions and asking more until the village maestro got flustered and made him sit in a corner. Hearing of this prodigy, Father Caviglia came to speak to Luca's grandparents about sending him to the seminary, one of the few options for poor boys with a quick mind. A deal was quickly struck.

Father Caviglia clasped his hands across his stomach, closed his eyes and lapsed into a gentle snore. Shrunk into his chair like that, with the rusty black cassock puddling around his ankles, he resembled a molting crow. Fighting the urge to yawn, Luca dutifully printed the title of his new assignment at the top of the paper.

P. CORNELI TACITI ANNALIVM LIBER SECVNDVS Liber III.

The sleepy lesson was interrupted by a knock on the rectory's front entrance across the hall. Luca heard the shuffling footsteps of Signora Scotti, the housekeeper who lived behind the rectory kitchen. Voices murmured and then Signora Scotti rapped on the door of the study.

Father Caviglia snapped awake. "Come in."

The housekeeper's wizened face poked around the edge of the door. "Father, you have a visitor. The military man. *Colonello* Orsini. He brought a rabbit for the stew pot."

"How kind. Send him in." Father Caviglia unfolded himself and swayed to his feet, panting a little from the exertion.

The door opened all the way. Signora Scotti shuffled aside, wiping her face with her ever-present dish towel.

The man who killed Luca's parents stepped into the study.

"*Colonello* Orsini," Father Caviglia murmured. "How good of you to call on me."

"Father, I apologize for intruding so late." He pressed the

priest's hand with reverence and exchanged kisses on the cheek before handing over a book. "Your library is such a luxury for an educated man in this place that I could not bear the thought of waiting another day. I wanted to return this and beg your leave to borrow another. I left the rabbit with your housekeeper. Shot just as dusk fell, not more than two hours ago. A small token of appreciation for sharing your library."

"Thank you, thank you. Bless you for your generosity." Father Caviglia indicated the bookcase by the window. "You are welcome to borrow anything."

Orsini noticed Luca sitting by the side of the desk, barely breathing as he hunched over the Latin text. "I'm interrupting you," Orsini said to Father Caviglia.

"The boy is preparing for his examination to enter the seminary."

"Ah." Orsini turned his attention to the bookcase.

Heart hammering, Luca waited for Father Caviglia to say the name Lombardo and for Orsini's eyes to open wide in surprised recall. Neither thing happened. Father Caviglia made no introductions. The military officer paid Luca no further attention.

The ancient priest called for Signora Scotti to bring another lamp as he and Orsini began discussing the borrowed book, which was returned to the correct shelf with care. The voices of the priest and the officer receded as they discussed Cicero and Cato the Younger, replaced inside Luca's head by the deafening buzz of a thousand angry bees.

Colonello Orsini. Colonel Orsini.

After twelve years, Orsini had barely changed except for more gold sprinkled on his military uniform. Even in the flickering glow of the oil lamps, the scar bending around his chin was clearly visible: a souvenir of conflict, a legacy of cruelty.

The mark of Cain so that Luca would know him when their paths crossed again.

Luca mechanically translated Tacitus. Orsini chose a new book, received a supplicant's blessing from Father Caviglia, and left with more apologies for interrupting the priest so late in the day.

"Who was that?" Luca asked after Father Caviglia had resettled himself behind the desk and the thunder of the visitor's horse had faded.

"*Colonnello* Humberto Orsini is the commander of the brigade at Spadola." Father Caviglia bristled with associated importance. "An educated man who appreciates a good library."

"Where does he live?" Luca heard himself ask. "With his soldiers?"

"No, no. He has a wonderful home." Father Caviglia clasped his hands. "Big and white, on the road to the Taverna dei Borboni. But empty. He has no wife, no children. Only art. A feast for the eyes and the soul."

"No wife, no children," Luca repeated numbly.

The priest made a theatrical gesture, the sleeve of his cassock flapping as his claw-like hand circled in mid-air. "Only a hunger for knowledge."

Two nights later, Luca walked all the way to the crossroads north of Spadola, passing the military barracks on the outskirts of the town. If he turned onto the other road, he'd pass the Taverna dei Borboni, a roadhouse for pilgrims heading south to the secluded Certosa di Serra San Bruno monastery founded by Saint Bruno.

Luca didn't turn. He kept walking. Soon Orsini's house emerged in the distance, just like Father Caviglia had described. A ghostly white square topped with terracotta tiles, silhouetted against the starry night sky.

The two-story house was set back from the road. Tall cypress trees rose like sentries on either side of the front elevation. A stable behind the house was bigger than the home of Luca's grandparents.

Unseen in the velvet blackness, Luca watched the house from a ragged row of trees that flanked the opposite side of the road. The night was unusually quiet. Insects whined but no chickens pecked at the dust, no goats bleated for attention.

No military guard paced the road in deference to the important officer inside.

A soft light glowed behind a window on the bottom floor, illuminating a single silhouette. Eventually the light moved to an upstairs window. When it went out, the house was completely dark.

Luca began the long trek back to Serra San Bruno.

He walked to Spadola the next night, too. Again, he watched the lights in the big white house. Orsini appeared to live a solitary life, reading on the first floor until late, then climbing the stairs to bed.

The third night Luca carefully extracted his father's gun from its hiding place in the loft of his grandparents' house.

After the deaths of his parents, Luca's grandfather gave him a bushel basket and told the 5-year-old to take what he wanted from the Lombardo house. Luca prayed for this to be a dream, prayed to hear his father's voice playing the counting game, but his grandfather just shoved him inside and told him to hurry.

There wasn't much of value inside the house that his mother called their nest. Luca played the counting game with himself as he filled the basket. Six books. Eight articles of clothing. Two napkins that his mother had embroidered. One leather portfolio with a gold crest. One gun.

The next day, Luca's grandfather burned the house down.

Luca moved into the loft of his grandparents' house. They never knew their house harbored the gun of a deserter, a crime for which they'd surely be punished if it became common knowledge.

Not even Enzo ever knew about the gun.

Luca carefully laid the gun on the straw pallet that served as his bed, rotated the chamber, and carefully extracted the six brass-jacketed bullets.

The scrape of heavy feet on the ladder to the loft made Luca whirl around. His grandfather's head came into view. Luca abruptly sat on the straw pallet to hide the gun.

"The priest told your grandmother that you didn't go for your lesson last night," his grandfather snapped.

Luca stared at his grandfather while a thousand fears flew through his head. Had someone seen him on the road to Spadola? Who else had Father Caviglia told?

He had no choice but to brazen it out. "I was there," Luca said.

"That's not what he said."

"Father Caviglia fell asleep." Luca nonchalantly placed his palms on the pallet alongside his thighs to keep the bullets from rolling off. "He does that sometimes while I write out the translations."

His grandfather narrowed his eyes. "You weren't with that Benedetto girl, were you?"

"I told you, Father Caviglia fell asleep." It was easy for Luca to infuse his voice with irritation. "He's so old he can't stay awake. Then he doesn't remember."

"Well, wake him up next time." Grumbling under his breath, Luca's grandfather backed down the ladder. His head disappeared below the level of the loft's floor.

Luca closed his eyes, hating that he had to lie about Father Caviglia. He didn't move until he heard his grandfather leave the house for his nightly dose of *grappa* at the *trattoria* with the other old men of the village.

He took off his shirt, tucked the gun into the waistband of his trousers, and tightened his suspenders over his bare chest so that the gun stayed in place. His trousers sagged as he slipped three bullets into each side pocket. Finally, he pulled his shirt over his suspenders so it covered the gun and his lumpy pockets, tied a blue bandana around his neck, clambered down the ladder and announced to his grandmother that he was heading to the rectory for his lesson with Father Caviglia.

When he got to the crossroads near the Taverna dei Borboni, Luca crouched in the shelter of the trees. Across the road, the big white house was quiet. Light brightened the same first floor window again, outlining a man's silhouette. Orsini was a man of regular habits.

Moonlight winked on the brass jackets of heavy rounds as Luca loaded the gun. With his right hand securing the gun concealed in his pocket, Luca crossed the road and pounded on the front door.

He expected a servant, but Orsini opened the door himself. He was silhouetted by a yellow light coming from the room behind him. The somber glow was absorbed by a dark stone floor, as if the interior of the house was a cave lit only by a dying fire.

"Can I help you, boy?" Orsini asked with no flicker of recognition.

"Father Caviglia sent me," Luca replied, despite a sudden dryness in his mouth.

"Is he unwell?" Orsini appeared genuinely alarmed by this late-night missive. "Does he need help?"

"No, no nothing like that." Luca's resolve wavered, almost undone by the man's spark of real concern.

"Then why are you here?

Luca licked his lips and remembered his lines. "Father Caviglia lent you a book, he said. But he needs it back so I said I would fetch it for him."

"Ah, of course." Orsini squinted at Luca. "You're his student, aren't you?"

"That's right."

"Come in." Orsini opened the door all the way. Luca could see that the *colonello* wasn't in uniform but wore the simple linen pants and loose shirt of a Calabrian peasant. The scar was still there, however, a malevolent white snake curled around his chin.

The mark of Cain.

Orsini frowned at Luca's hesitation. The snake tightened against the shadow of his beard. "What's the matter?"

"May I have some water?" Luca asked hastily. His hand

tightened on the gun in his pocket.

"Yes, I expect you've had a long walk. Come with me."

Orsini led Luca into a room similar to Father Caviglia's study in the rectory, but three times as big and a hundred times richer. A patchwork of carpets with foreign designs covered the stone floor and anchored a big desk scattered with papers. A silver tray held the remains of a meal.

An ornate carriage clock dominated a wooden mantle that was so carved with cherubs and lavished in gold that it might have been an altar. Magnificent horses gazed out from a dozen oil paintings, creating a floor to ceiling equine tapestry of dappled black, moody browns, and gilt frames against walls washed with burnt umber.

Luca couldn't help marveling at so many beautiful things. "The paintings . . ." He trailed off, out of words.

"You may look at them." Orsini opened a cabinet, removed a glass, and poured water into it from a silver pitcher on the tray. Instead of offering the water to Luca, Orsini left the glass on the tray, sat behind the desk, and found a clean sheet of paper with a gold crest at the top.

The same military crest that decorated Matteo Lombardo's leather portfolio.

Luca took a sip of water, holding the glass in his left hand. The gun in his right pocket weighed more than a millstone. Orsini began scratching out a missive beginning with the words *Esteemed Father Caviglia.*

"My name is Gianluca Lombardo." Luca's voice cracked but his hand was steady as he returned the glass of water to the tray. "My father was Matteo Lombardo. My mother was named Viola."

"No doubt they are proud that their son is to become a priest," Orsini replied absently as he continued to write.

"They're both dead," Luca said flatly. "You killed them."

Orsini looked up and saw Matteo Lombardo's revolver pointed at his heart.

"What's this?" Orsini frowned. "A robbery?"

"My father was *Primo Capitano* Matteo Lombardo," Luca said. "An officer, like you. Executed as a deserter by your firing squad."

"When?" Orsini put down his pen.

Had Orsini killed so many that he no longer remembered their names? "Twelve years ago," Luca answered. "In Serra San Bruno."

"You're mistaken." Orsini spoke calmly. He capped his inkwell but kept his eye on the unwavering gun in Luca's hand.

"You found Matteo Lombardo in my grandfather's olive grove." Luca stepped closer to the desk. "Your horses trampled everything. Scared everyone into submission. Then you took my father, tied him to a tree and shot him."

Orsini made a show of slowly rifling through the papers on the desk. "If your father was an officer, he knew that execution is the punishment for desertion."

"I think you remember him." Luca's grip on the revolver was still remarkably steady. "After all, you must have hunted him for a long time. *Primo Capitano* Matteo Lombardo deserted years before you found him. Long enough to marry and have a son. I was just a child when you killed him."

"Matteo Lombardo." Orsini slowly drew out the name, his hands now motionless on the desk. "No, the name means nothing to me."

"What about Viola Lombardo? Why did you kill her, too?"

"You understand nothing of a soldier's duties," Orsini said contemptuously. "Get out of my house. If your parents are dead, you can pray for their souls in Purgatory when you become a priest."

"You remember them," Luca said. Everything in the softly lit home took on a sharper, colder edge. "I can see it in your eyes."

"These names mean nothing to me," Orsini snapped.

"You remember killing him. Killing her, too, when she cursed you."

"Who are you to come into my house like this?" Orsini leaped to his feet, no longer concerned about Luca's gun. "A deserter's brat? A common laborer from the olive groves with dirt under your fingernails?"

"Get on your knees," Luca said. He came around the side of the desk.

Orsini gave a bitterly incredulous laugh. "I'm not going to kneel to you. You're a boy with a deserter's gun. Get out of my house now and I'll forget this ever happened."

"Get on your knees," Luca repeated. "Another man would kill you. I'm giving you the chance to get on your knees and ask for my forgiveness."

"Ask forgiveness from the spawn of a deserter and a whore who spread her legs for the first man she saw who wasn't a Calabrian monkey?" Orsini snarled. "I should have made her spread her legs for me first."

Something silver flashed in the man's hand. Luca jerked away but Orsini's blade went under the gun and plunged deep. As warm dark blood bloomed across his shirt and pain dazzled his vision, Luca stumbled backward into the wall of paintings. Orsini came after him, knife poised to stab once again, face contorted in a snarling smile at his cornered prey.

Luca pulled the trigger.

The noise was deafening. Orsini swallowed the bullet. The back of his head blew off. His body collapsed onto the carpet.

Luca's ears rang as the gun's recoil generated spasms of pain. He realized that Orsini's silver knife protruded from his own chest.

For an excruciating minute, all Luca could do was gulp air and let the room swim around him. When the world was straight again, he braced himself and yanked out the knife. His ribs screamed and he sank to his knees as the pain threatened to swamp him. When his vision cleared, he clamped his left hand to his side and forced himself to look at the man he'd just murdered.

Orsini lay on his back on the elegant carpet. Part of his jaw was gone and his eyes stared sightlessly at the ceiling. The desk was covered in blood and grey matter.

With equine disinterest, the horses on the walls watched Luca weep at the enormity of his mortal sin, their framed splendor untouched by violence.

Outside the big white house, all was perfect stillness. The *Carabinieri* police didn't come to arrest him. No soldier appeared from the barracks to investigate a gunshot. Either the house was too remote, his soldiers were all drunk, or no one cared.

The clock chimed midnight. Luca hauled himself to his feet, finally able to think clearly. Moving slowly, he mounted the stairs. He found a clean shirt in Orsini's bedroom, as well as a length of linen to use as a bandage. Orsini's own Army revolver was in a chest by the side of the bed. It was loaded.

Luca brought it back to the study, extracted one bullet, pressed the gun into Orsini's dead hand with a forefinger curled around the trigger.

Fighting the pain in his side from the two stab wounds, he cleaned the thin blade Orsini apparently had used as a letter opener, and left it on the desk. He burned his bloody shirt and Orsini's letter to Father Caviglia in a kitchen pot before scrounging some ham and cheese from the larder. The food was fuel for the trek back to Serra San Bruno, although part of Luca was too ashamed to go back.

He had not intended to kill Orsini, but he had. The guilt was enormous, yet he also felt a sense of justice delivered and that made him no better than Orsini. Luca knew he'd carry a double burden of mortal sin. One for killing Orsini and another for being unrepentant.

It took less than a day for the news to jump from Spadola to Serra San Bruno. The commander of the brigade had taken his own life. For two days, it was all anyone talked about in the village. The gossips speculated that Orsini had succumbed to his own vices. No doubt, he was a gambler or in trouble with a woman.

A soldier returned Father Caviglia's book, but the poor priest was distraught. As a suicide, *Colonello* Orsini could not be buried in sanctified ground.

Luca didn't try to see Rafaella. He did his chores with his ribs wrapped in Orsini's sheet and translated Tacitus in Father Caviglia's study.

Five days passed. Orsini was buried. No one came to arrest

Luca.

Long after his grandfather returned from the village and his grandparents were snoring peacefully in their bedroom, Luca left the house with the gun once more tucked into the waistband of his trousers under his shirt. This time, his destination was the *trattoria.*

It was the center of life for the men of the village when the sun went down. Tables and chairs spilled out onto the street. Men nursed glasses of red wine, played chess, and ogled the young women who strolled across the village square pretending they weren't there to be noticed. Rafaella was never among them. Her father and brothers guarded her too closely to permit such loose behavior.

Luca threaded his way past the tables fronting the square. A few men nodded at him because they knew his grandfather, but most avoided acknowledging the deserter's son. No matter how many years went by, the village of Serra San Bruno would always consider Matteo's crime to be a sin that clung to his son.

Inside the *trattoria*, a blue cloud from cigars and cigarettes hung in the air. A bar ran the length of one smoke-streaked stucco wall. Men in work shirts and dungarees, smelling of honest sweat and Calabrian dirt, leaned on the wooden surface and nursed short glasses of red wine as they bickered over women and priests and taxes levied by the government in Rome.

The person he was looking for wasn't there. Luca found a space at the bar and asked for a glass of red wine and a biscotti. When the glass and plate were put in front of him, he dipped the twice-baked almond cookie into the wine to soften it. He ate it slowly, determined to ignore the disapproving glances of the old men, the ache in his side or the gun digging into his stomach. With one half of his brain, he counted heads, glasses, and cracks in the walls. With the other half he counted the minutes and watched the doorway.

He'd almost given up hope when Ettore Scarpa and his gang swaggered in. Luca raised a hand and Ettore favored him with a nod.

"Hey, Luca." Ettore was the same age as Luca's cousin Enzo. With his slick pompadour and a pock-marked face, Ettore was well known in Serra San Bruno. Girls were attracted to his bold talk and pockets full of *lira*, but mothers pulled their daughters inside when he passed. The older men grumbled about Ettore and his gang but there was jealousy in their voices.

The Scarpa men were smugglers. If a man in Serra San Bruno needed a prostitute, a smoke, or a loan, he went to a Scarpa. A few times a year, Luca's grandfather sold cheese to Ettore's father and was paid in cigarettes.

The cigarettes were never smoked. They were too valuable as currency to pay off the tax collector.

The Scarpas even did business with Sicilians, the gossips said in low, furtive voices. Sicily, the island perpetually kicked by Calabria into the Mediterranean, was loaded with criminals and scoundrels with dirty fingers everywhere. Joseph Petrosino, a famous policeman from America, was gunned down in Palermo not so many years ago, blackening the island's eye for all time.

"Can I talk to you?" Luca murmured to Ettore.

"Sure, sure."

"Not here."

Ettore shrugged. "Sure."

Luca followed him out of the *trattoria* and down a skinny alley. Ettore stopped at a two-story house on the southern edge of the village and climbed a crude wooden ladder braced against the wall. With his ribs on fire and one hand at his waistband to safeguard the gun, Luca followed him up the ladder. The flat roof of the house was partially covered by a canvas canopy to create a shelter from the sun. Now at night, the effect was of a subterranean cave suspended in the sky and Ettore swaggered like a swarthy sultan in charge of all he saw.

Luca slowly drew out his father's revolver. "How much will you give me for this?"

Ettore took the gun and walked to the overhanging edge of the canopy where moonlight played over the smooth metal. "Where did you get it?"

"It was my father's."

Ettore let out a low whistle. "A genuine Army pistol."

"It's for sale," Luca said.

"But it's a deserter's gun." Ettore hefted the revolver and his teeth flashed white in a knowing grin. "Okay, Luca. I like you. Six hundred *lira*."

"A thousand," Luca countered.

"A thousand?" Ettore gave a low laugh but he didn't give the gun back. "What does a priest need with a thousand *lira*? I'll pay you seven hundred."

Luca knew Ettore wanted the gun. "Nine hundred fifty."

"Seven hundred."

Luca took the bullets out of his pocket, knowing that it was harder to find ammunition than it was to find weapons. "Maybe you want these, too."

Surprise flashed across Ettore's face at the six brass-jacketed rounds in Luca's hand. Five from his father's gun and one from Orsini's.

They haggled, trading numbers back and forth until they settled on 1200 *lira* for both the gun and ammunition. It was enough.

With the moon to guide him and his pockets heavy with the money, Luca slipped through the lemon and orange groves of the Benedetto family. A chorus of dogs met him as he approached the farm. The lamps were still lit in the kitchen.

Everyone was at home, which meant that Luca had to ask Rafaella's father for her hand in marriage in front of her mother and five brothers, as well as a beaming Rafaella.

He'd give her a good home in America, he promised. A good life. He and Rafaella would join his cousin Enzo, who had a wife and a farm of his own now. Rafaella's mother sobbed openly as her father grudgingly consented, his eyes on the money for passenger fares across the ocean. Yes, Luca could marry his daughter. Take her away to the land of opportunity, where so many others went.

They knew Luca would inherit nothing with which to provide a life for a family. Nor could the Benedetto farm support another mouth to feed and the children sure to follow. They were already among the poorest in Serra San Bruno, with too many sons and so little land.

"My cousin Enzo's farm is in a place called Lido, in New York." Luca told them about Enzo's letters describing land that was so rich it was black and watered by the heavens every week. This wasn't the dry dusty land in Calabria, but land for cows to graze on and fed by clear water from a river called

Mohawk. Anything would grow there. Garlic, onions, tomatoes the size of a man's head. Again and again, Luca reassured Rafaella's parents of the good life their daughter would have.

Father Caviglia tried to put a stop to it, but Luca and Rafaella married four months later.

She was pregnant when they left Serra San Bruno, bound for the ship that would take them to America.

April 1919

Behind Conover's Saloon in the Bowery neighborhood
New York City, New York

The crowd roared drunken approval as his opponent's fist pitched Luca into the first line of cheering onlookers. His head swam as they hurled him back into the circle where Plugger Horan waited for another go at his opponent.

Blood streamed out of Plugger's swollen nose and his chest heaved like a bellows, but the big Irishman was undefeated. No Italian punk was going to break his winning streak.

Luca was undefeated, too, but if he didn't come up with an idea, Plugger was going to tear him apart. The big Irishman was easily four inches taller and had fists like bricks. He weighed a good thirty pounds more than Luca, although it was hard to say how much of that weight was beer and how much was muscle.

The bare-knuckled fights were held behind Conover's Saloon on Delancey Street, in the heart of the Irish slums and a long walk from the Italian tenements clustered around Mulberry and Elizabeth Streets to the west. No ring, no neutral corners, no rules, just a shouting circle of men cheering and drinking and betting on their favored fighter.

After Luca decked a would-be thief who aimed to help himself to Rafaella's purse, Finn Conover himself sought him out to fight. Twenty dollars if Luca held out more than five minutes. Seventy-five if he knocked out his opponent, the only way to win. So far Luca had won three fights, earning 225 dollars.

But Plugger was a real crowd pleaser. Tonight's stakes were nearly triple the usual. The winner of this fight would make 200 dollars and Luca needed the money more than he needed air to breathe. Rafaella was sick, the baby was on the way, he had no job, and everything in America cost too much.

"Had enough, wop?" Plugger panted. "Come here so I can end you."

Luca sidestepped around the circle, trying to clear his head and come up with a plan. At the beginning of the fight, the big Irishman had danced like a jackrabbit, weaving and skipping from side to side. Now he stood still, shoulders hunched to the left and arms down. Both fists were smeared with his own blood.

Luca's chest ached, his muscles quivered, and one eye was nearly swollen shut. But unlike Plugger, he could still breathe easily, drawing in gusts of air thick with the stink of sour beer and old piss. Not yet 20 years old and fists up with the resiliency of youth, he maneuvered around the ring of jeering, shouting men, and decided he had one advantage over Plugger.

La testa dura.

Luca hurled himself across the circle with the force of a locomotive and rammed Plugger in the chest with his head, catapulting the bigger man into the turbulent crowd. Loud enough to be heard above the ensuing roar, Plugger's ribs gave a thunderous crack. The man's chest caved in so suddenly that Luca almost lost his balance.

Plugger stayed on his feet by cranking an elbow around Luca's neck and trapping him close. Gasping for air, with stars twinkling before his eyes, Luca battered Plugger's ribcage with fists like pistons powering a runaway train.

The big Irishman turned into a wheezing, wobbling elephant. His knees buckled as blow after blow smashed into his torso. With his elbow still locked around Luca's neck, Plugger pitched backward. The world tilted as Luca went with him.

The ground shook when they hit. The crowd hollered. Spit bubbled out of Plugger's mouth.

With the crowd surging and his ears ringing, Luca got to one knee and continued to hammer both fists into Plugger's side. The big man curled up, moaning. Luca finished him with a two-handed wrecking ball blow to the jaw that bounced Plugger's head against the dirt. The big man's eyes rolled back and his arms flopped to his sides. Bloody froth spewed out of his mouth and nose, along with the stench of defeat.

Finn Conover jumped into the circle and roared out the count. The crowd shouted at the champ to get up, Irish brogues rising above the clamor and competing with Italian approval for Luca. At the count of ten, Finn grabbed Luca's arm and raised it over his head. "Undefeated!" Finn bellowed.

It was one of the few words of English that Luca had learned since coming to America.

An hour later, Finn paid Luca his winnings in the back room of the saloon, minus his so-called promotional fee and a dollar for a beer and a pickled egg. With his left eye swollen shut and knuckles the size of eggplants, Luca started home with Olindo Pellegrini and Sal Graziano, new friends who lived in the same tenement on Mulberry Street. For five dollars each, they acted as bodyguards. If a tired champ was stupid enough to walk the streets alone, it would be easy to jump him and steal his winnings. Doubly tempting if the champ was a stupid Italian wop who'd just defeated an Irish fighter in the Irish stronghold of the Bowery.

Luca had not intended to stay in New York City, but the passage across the Atlantic in steerage had been exceptionally hard on Rafaella. Her pregnancy meant that she was either crying for her mother or vomiting all the time. It started when they left Reggio di Calabria, the first stop on the journey from Serra San Bruno. There they boarded a ferry to Genoa. As the coast of Calabria receded into the distance, Rafaella cried so hard she made herself sick.

Genoa was a nightmare. Almost dragging Rafaella behind him, Luca found them a place to stay for the three nights before the ship left for America. She wrote her mother a last letter before they boarded and found their berths in the windowless compartment crammed with almost a hundred other Italian immigrants seeking a better life. The ventilation couldn't keep up with the number of unwashed bodies and the compartment stank, aggravating Rafaella past the breaking point. Luca's sense of purpose and adventure was shaken by his perpetually sobbing young wife.

Rescue came in the form of fellow immigrant Alma Pellegrini, a midwife from Crotone on the Ionian coast. Alma took Rafaella under her wing and made her as comfortable as possible under the circumstances. By the time the young couple got through Ellis Island, Rafaella was adamant that they stay near Alma until the baby was born. They could go to Lido after that.

Olindo and Alma Pellegrini elected to stay in New York

City where they had relatives. So Luca reluctantly wrote to Enzo to say that they were delayed, and rented a room in the same tenement in lower Manhattan. The Little Italy neighborhood was an enormous enclave of recently arrived Italians, bookended by the churches of St. Anthony of Padua on Sullivan Street and Our Lady of Pompeii on Bleecker.

Luca hated it there. Tenement life, with its crowds of people living on top of each other, was no place to make a home. The constant churn was like nothing Luca had ever known before. Not even the feast day of Saint Bruno was as raucously noisy as every day in New York City. At all hours of the day the rushing energy of the city assaulted him. The air was perpetually full of sound and smell, starting with the flap of wet laundry hanging from every window of the tall brick tenement buildings. Pushcart vendors hawked their prices, newsboys yelled the headlines, and horse-drawn wagons carrying every good imaginable clattered up and down the streets. Even automobiles honked their way through the chaos.

The air was clammy and the rivers encircling the city were awash in factory filth. The big city smelled sour, spoiled, unbearable. Little Italy was a rickety jumble of tenements, rats, and thieves looking to exploit a newcomer's ignorance and dismay.

Luca found it hard to breathe, just from the sheer weight of humanity pressing on him from all sides. Everyone shouted for a newspaper, to sell fruit, or entice customers into the many barber shops.

He hoped Lido was different. Surely all of America wasn't this noisy, this suffocating. He longed to leave.

Their rented room was on the third floor, with a window,

a bed, a table, and two chairs. The bathroom was down the hall and shared with five other families. The walls between their room and the neighboring apartments were so thin, they might as well have been invisible. Luca could hear everything said on either side.

The Pellegrini family lived on the first floor but Alma was in and out of their room. As Rafaella's stomach got bigger, the rest of her got thinner. She cried and coughed at night and was exhausted all the time. When it rained she complained that the damp walls made her cold.

Luca did what he could to keep her spirits up, but mostly he looked for work.

Men congregated at designated street corners in the neighborhood to wait for foremen who needed day laborers to build the ever-growing America. Bricklayers and stonemasons were in demand. Those skills were rare. But men who had worked the land in Italy had no special skills to offer and scrambled to find enough work to feed their families. Luca picked up jobs here and there, carrying bricks or water on construction sites, but was often passed over in favor of older men with more mouths to feed. Soon, he was faced with the choice of selling fruit from a pushcart like Olindo or vying for business as one of the dozens of shoeshine boys that roamed Manhattan.

A photographer on Mulberry Street helped him put off the decision, paying Luca the princely sum of twenty dollars to pose for a picture. "The ladies will stop to look," the man said, eying Luca in the way his grandfather used to assess new goats. "They all want to see a handsome man, eh?"

In short order, Luca found himself draped in a secondhand

suit two sizes too big with his hair neatly combed, posed on a leather bench in front of the camera tripod. When the photographer held up the sulfur flash and ordered Luca to think happy thoughts, his father's counting game was the first thing that came to mind.

Luca saw the portrait a few days later. Resplendent in an oval frame, he was a sepia-toned stranger swimming in wool, the shirt collar and tie hanging limply around his neck. But even as he stood dumbly in front of the window lettered with the photographer's name, two women stopped to gawk at the portrait.

"He's somebody famous," one said. "Look at that face."

"Caruso." The other woman reverently named the most famous opera singer Italy ever produced. "That has to be a young Caruso."

Before Luca could say anything, the photographer popped out of the studio door and said yes, he had the greatest honor to photograph Enrico Caruso as a young man. Five minutes later, each woman put a deposit down on a family portrait.

Before the photographer's money was all spent, Luca won his first fight for Finn Conover.

It was 16 blocks from the Bowery to Mulberry Street. Twilight softened the clutter of advertising signs and sharp-edged buildings, but the rush of noise that marked every passing day continued unabated. This was the city that never slept.

The three men stopped along the way. Rafaella's cough had been worse of late. Luca spent some of his winnings on bananas and honey at Carlucci's and a sack of peppermints at Rizzo's candy shop before they made it to their row of four-story tenement houses on Mulberry Street.

As usual, the scrum of children playing in front shouted at Luca as they saw the men approach. Between rumors that he was the spitting image of a young Enrico Caruso and being the local bare-knuckle champion, Luca had acquired the status of a minor celebrity.

"Luca! Did you win?"

With a grin, Luca handed out the peppermints from Rizzo's. The kids fell on them like wolves and the three men went inside.

Alma Pellegrini met them on the stair landing. "The baby came," she said shortly.

Luca gaped at her. "You said next month."

"She coughed it out," Alma said with a shrug that spoke of too many babies, too many hard births.

"It is a boy or girl?" Luca asked.

"A boy."

Luca raced up the stairs two at a time, his aches and pains from the fight instantly forgotten. Rafaella was in the bed, the baby wrapped in a swaddling blanket and tucked into the crook of her arm. The pillow was stained with sweat and the blood Rafaella sometimes coughed up.

"Did you win?" she asked groggily.

"I won." Luca dropped the bag of fruit and knelt by the bed. He marveled at the baby, so small and red and wrinkled, eyes shut tight. "You made a baby."

Rafaella mustered a tired smile.

"Now, you see," Luca said. He pushed sweaty hair off Rafaella's forehead. "Everything will be good. The baby is here. We have money. You won't be sick anymore."

Three days later, both Rafaella and the baby were dead.

Spanish influenza, the doctor had said gravely before giving Rafaella laudanum to ease her incessant coughing. The disease, mostly contained the year before, swept through the Mulberry Street tenements like wildfire. Alma told Luca to keep Rafaella cool with damp cloths on her forehead, but the fever still raged.

The baby boy died before Rafaella slipped away from Luca, delirious and gasping for hours before her final, labored breath. Luca unconsciously counted each rattling intake of air. Four thousand and twelve breaths. Four thousand and twelve eternities waiting for her to die.

Four thousand and twelve breaths that told him this was punishment for murdering Orsini and getting married in a church while in a state of mortal sin.

Like a sleepwalker, Luca said nothing as workers from the New York City Department of Public Health collected the bodies to be buried along with the rest of the penniless immigrants who died of influenza that week. He said nothing as he sent a simple five-word telegram to Enzo in Lido.

The second telegram was harder to write. He'd promised to give Rafaella a good life. Instead, he had to tell her parents in Serra San Bruno that she and the baby were dead.

Once the telegrams were sent, Luca gave all of Rafaella's meager wardrobe to Alma, packed what was left, and bought a train ticket.

September 1920

The farm of Enzo and Rosaria Russo on Bell Road
Lido, New York

"I didn't come all this way to have nothing," Luca said.

"We'll buy more land," Enzo said. "The farm can belong to both of us."

They were shucking corn on the front steps of the farmhouse where Enzo and his wife Rosaria lived with their toddler son and infant daughter. Sunshine warmed the autumn day. Across Bell Road, maple trees threw scarlet and caramel into a robin's egg sky.

For the past year, Luca had slept in the musty unfinished attic, in the bed that Enzo had bought for him and Rafaella, hearing birds thrash on the roof and awakening to daylight shining through the chinks in the clapboards. At night he did more pacing than sleeping, flinching when one of the children below cried out. The pain of his loss stabbed more deeply than Orsini's knife ever did.

The farm was south of Lido, along a country road that approached the Mohawk River and petered out along the riverbank. The closest neighbor was the big Genovese farm a mile down the road. The only reading material in the house was a Bible, a handbook of American laws for immigrants, and an English dictionary.

When they weren't working, Enzo and Teresa were consumed with their children, each other, and the mortgage on the farm.

Work was Luca's salvation. The farm boasted two cows, three pigs, a flock of chickens, and a few acres of root vegetables Enzo sold to stores in Lido. Luca did whatever Enzo needed done, from building a chicken coop to chopping a hoe between rows of carrots and beets. He milked the cows, slopped the hogs, picked vegetables, counted weeds and stones, on and on, until he was exhausted enough to sleep.

Rosaria said once that he was too young to live like a hermit. Her words were meant as encouragement, but provoked an unexpected surge of despair and anger. Luca rushed away from the dinner table and ran through the field to the very edge of his sanity. There he waited, trembling with uncontrollable emotion, until the sound of Rafaella's labored breaths in his mind faded away, and the night was once again full of stars and chilly air and the chirp of crickets. Rosaria never said anything like that again, but he knew that she watched him.

"I don't want to be a farmer anymore," Luca heard himself say as he tore the silk off an ear of corn.

Enzo's face creased in surprise and hurt.

"Before, with Rafaella," Luca went on lamely. "It was what she wanted. It was all she knew. If she was here, it would be different."

"What do you want to do?"

"I don't know." Luca tossed the ear of corn into the bushel on the porch.

He didn't know anything except that he could not keep living in Enzo's attic, with the ghost of Rafaella floating through his dreams and the sin of killing Orsini tugging at his conscience. All the way from Calabria to never have nothing more than this?

Two days later, Enzo brought home a newspaper from a quick trip into Lido. The *Lido Daily Clipper* had a page that listed available jobs. Enzo translated one that stood out.

HELP WANTED
Handyman needed for growing establishment.
Fair wage. See Vito Spinelli.
Inquire before 10 am. 601 Hamilton Street.

"Everyone knows Vito," Enzo said. "He runs a nice place."

With the newspaper tucked under his arm, Luca walked into Lido the next morning and found the address. The two-story brick building occupied half a block along Hamilton Street, a busy thoroughfare that ran through the Italian enclave known as East Lido, bounded by Saint Rocco's Catholic Church on one end and the Lido Premium Copper and Brass Rolling Mill on the other. Enzo and Teresa attended Mass at Saint Rocco's every Sunday morning, along with every other Italian in Lido.

Except Luca, who had not been in a church since Rafaella and the baby died.

East Lido was bustling that morning. Automobiles rumbled up and down Hamilton Street as pedestrians churned along the sidewalks in front of the stout brick buildings that lined it on both sides. Many on the street were women with baskets over their arms, doing the day's shopping at the multitude of stores and stalls. Luca saw signs in English and Italian for Red's Butcher Shop, the Bella Napoli Pastry Shop, a glovemaker, a shoe store, a secondhand clothing shop, and dozens of other businesses.

The skinny streets snaking north from Hamilton Street were crowded with narrow two-story clapboard residences. Laundry flapped from first and second-floor porches, reminding Luca of the Mulberry Street tenements. Each house was no doubt filled to bursting with multiple families.

The building at 601 Hamilton Street had two identical doors, each sporting a wavy glass window shaded by a black and white striped awning. Between the two doors, a big window proclaimed *GALLIANO CLUB est. 1912* in gold letters that arched across the plate glass. Coming closer, Luca saw gilt numbers painted on the glass inset of each door. The door on the right was number 601 and the one on the left was 601½.

He pushed open the door on the right and stepped into a small vestibule. A shoulder-height wall was just ahead, enclosing the space but not cutting it off from the room beyond. A flagstone floor, a bench on one side and a row of hooks for coats made it into a cozy nook. A broom stood in a corner.

Passing through the vestibule, Luca emerged into a large saloon. His eye was immediately drawn to display of liquor bottles glittering against a mirrored wall above a dark mahogany bar. The bar ran the length of the room, complete with elaborate decorative molding and a gleaming brass foot rail. A dozen leather-topped stools suggested customers who stayed long enough to need a comfortable perch.

An enormous bottle of Liquore Galliano, as tall as Luca but as thin as a reed where it tapered at the top, occupied pride of place in the center of the display of bottles. The chartreuse yellow liqueur glowed like a beacon; both reflected by the mirror behind and spotlighted from above by the electric lights hanging from the pressed tin ceiling. Luca had never seen a bottle that large. It would take at least four men to lift and pour it.

Almost hidden by the magnificent bar, a parallel work counter jammed against the wall was laden with an untidy clutter of glasses, plates, loaves of bread and enormous jars of pickled eggs and onions. Centered under the Liquore Galliano, a big brass cash register promised the jingle of coins.

The rest of the saloon was simply decorated. Above wainscotting painted a midnight green, the white walls showed off a handful of framed photographs and sports pennants. More than a dozen square tables and bentwood chairs filled the middle of the space. The parquet floors needed polishing.

The place smelled of coffee and salami, with a generous helping of stale smoke.

A short, thickset man with marcelled hair and a generous mustache appeared at the far end of the saloon and said something in English too fast for Luca to understand.

Luca snatched the cap off his head. "*Sono qui per lavoro*," he said. *I am here for work.*

"I'm Vito Spinelli." Vito spoke in Italian, his voice gruff but not unkind.

"My name is Luca Lombardo. I'm here about the job in the newspaper."

The two men sized each other up, Luca taking in Vito's quality three-piece suit and gold watch chain stretched over an ample belly, as the other man assessed the shapeless wool trousers, limp linen shirt, and frayed jacket that practically shouted Luca's status as a recent immigrant.

"You don't speak English?" Vito asked, still speaking in Italian.

Luca twisted his cap in his hands. "I'm learning."

"From Calabria," Vito prompted, no doubt recognizing the regional accent.

Luca nodded. "Serra San Bruno."

"Can you read?"

"Yes." Luca showed the other man the circled ad in the *Lido Daily Clipper*. "My cousin is Enzo Russo. He says you're a good man. That this is a good place."

Vito fingered his mustache. Luca squared his shoulders and tried to look older.

"You understand about Prohibition?" Vito asked. He gestured to the immense bottle of Liquore Galliano above the bar. "That's for show. No liquor sales until Prohibition is done."

"Will it be done soon?"

"I hope not." Vito gave a short laugh. "I like to make money."

"I don't understand."

"This is a members-only club. They pay dues and can come in any time for a cup of coffee or a sandwich. Most work at the Lido Premium mill. When they come in, they're thirsty. Thirsty like men who work hard, you understand?"

Luca nodded, although he wasn't sure what Vito meant.

"You look strong enough," Vito said, abruptly changing the subject. "How much can you lift?"

"I'm strong enough to work a full day and not complain. I'll give you good value for your money, Mr. Spinelli."

The mustache twitched. "You're a bold one."

"I'm honest," Luca said.

Vito rubbed his mustache again. "Let's see how you do."

He led Luca through the saloon and down a central hallway, pointing out things as they went. On the right, a small kitchen was even more haphazard than the work counter behind the bar. A pool room sported two tables, a rack of cues, and a chalkboard for keeping score. To the left, sandwiched between the saloon and Vito's office at the back of the building, was a closet-sized library with a desk and two overstuffed chairs. A treasure trove of newspapers waited to be read, draped over slotted wooden poles held by a rack that resembled a small hollow table. Most of the papers were in Italian, although Luca recognized the masthead of the *Lido Daily Clipper*.

Vito opened a door in a niche next to the kitchen to reveal a shallow pantry filled with food tins and preserves in mason jars. He gave Luca a slow wink and pressed on two of the shelves, prompting a metallic click. The entire pantry swung to the side.

"This is where we store everything," Vito said. "It's cool all the time. You have to be strong enough to bring it up."

Cold air billowed from a dark abyss. Vito pulled a cord dangling just inside and an electric light revealed a deep cellar. The temperature dropped with every step down the unfinished wooden stairs.

A sloping dirt floor and a ceiling of exposed joists supported the upper stories. Boxes and barrels were piled up in no discernable arrangement, all but obscuring a service door at the far end.

"Can you lift that?" Vito pointed to a wooden barrel the size of Enzo's prize pig. "Bring it upstairs.

Luca easily hefted the barrel onto his shoulder although the center of gravity shifted as the contents sloshed from side to side. A strong yeasty smell permeated the wooden staves. "Is this beer?"

"Damn right it's beer," Vito said. "I paid thirty dollars for it from the Antonelli brothers."

"It's short by at least twenty percent," Luca said. "But there's enough that if you sell it at 50 cents a glass, you'll triple your investment."

Vito's mustache quivered and his eyes popped. "Are you some sort of mathematician?"

By late evening, the barrel was empty, and Luca had memorized the names of over 75 club members who came in that day. Vito got another shock when Luca told him exactly how much was in the cash register without having to count the money.

"I'm hiring a handyman," Vito said suspiciously. "You leave the business side to me."

"Do I have the job?"

"Twelve dollars a week. Club opens at 11:00. Closed on Sunday. You can have sandwiches and coffee but you pay for your beer and liquor same as everybody else. And you keep your mouth shut, understand?"

Luca left Enzo and Rosaria with the promise to return every Sunday to help with farm chores. He rented a room in a boarding house a few blocks from the club and plunged into the new job with a will.

In short order, he fixed broken furniture, became a self-taught electrician, organized the work counter and cellar, cleaned the place from top to bottom and took over the task of buying the newspapers and keeping the library organized. Luca helped semi-literate members who wanted to send money orders or telegrams back to the old country, stocking the library with forms from Western Union and the Post Office. When the Antonelli brothers showed up with partially filled barrels of beer, Luca had a quiet conversation with them. The next time, the barrels were full.

Guido Serra, the stodgy and semi-literate doorman who presided over the vestibule, watched all the progress with something approaching hero worship.

True to his promise, every Sunday Luca went back to the farm to help Enzo and Rosaria. In time, the children's cries were no more than reminders of his cousin's good fortune.

His generous salary, however, was a heavy burden. After the first month, Luca opened an account at the big First National Bank of Lido and arranged for a money transfer to an account at the Bank of Napoli in the name of Rafaella's father. Half of his salary was Rafaella's share of the good life he'd promised her parents. He sent the money the second month, too, and the third, and then every month.

Virtually every Italian male living in East Lido was a member of the club. Most worked at the Lido Premium mill on the far end of Hamilton Street. Starting at 7:00 am, the steam whistle shrilled a note that interrupted conversations up and down the street. The resolute howl started the workday, marked lunch and breaks, and sent men home from the largest mill in New York. Within its stout brick walls, molten ore was shaped into copper and brass for America's bridges, ship hulls, railroad carriages, and power grids.

For the workers at Lido Premium, the whistle was a summons to build and sweat and prosper. For Luca, it was a clarion call to leave his sins behind.

As the months rolled by, he took on more tasks without being asked. Vito didn't object. In addition to handyman duties, Luca also managed the food deliveries, made sandwiches, kept track of dues, and recruited more members.

During the day, those who dropped in for a cup of coffee or read the newspaper weren't mill workers but farmers like Enzo, old-timers who played cards or chess all afternoon, and business owners in East Lido. The Galliano Club came alive in the evenings.

Once the last whistle of the day sounded, club members arrived in two thirsty waves. The first wave rushed in, still in their stained and sweaty dungarees, for a glass of beer or two before going home for dinner. The second wave went home first, ate supper with their family, and surged into the club later, much the same way Luca's grandfather went to Serra San Bruno's *trattoria* in the evenings.

It didn't take long for Luca to discover that the Galliano Club was the hub of most community events in East Lido, too, from holiday raffles to the May Day picnic. It took even less time for news to get around that Luca was single, literate, and had all his teeth. Members sheepishly mentioned that their wives wanted to meet him. Maybe she could introduce Luca to a cousin or a sister at Sunday supper or a dance at Saint Rocco's. Even his new landlady, Mrs. Esposito, tried unsuccessfully to play matchmaker.

He politely refused all invitations, giving the honest

excuse that he helped his cousin Enzo on his only day off. The tragedy of Rafaella and the baby remained private.

Luca continued to send half his salary to the Bank of Napoli every month and imagined what the gossips in Serra San Bruno were saying. *The traitor's son took poor Rafaella Benedetto away to die in America. Now he sends money, trying to atone for his sins.*

They were right, although the village gossips would never know the whole story.

The only woman in East Lido who didn't want to be a matchmaker was Vito's wife Louise, who rarely came into the club even though she and Vito lived in the apartment upstairs. The door on the left with the address of 601½ Hamilton Street opened to stairs leading directly to the second floor. There was no other access. Vito said they built the separation on purpose. Louise didn't want club members sneaking up the back stairs and getting into their apartment.

Vito's wife was the opposite of her husband. Louise was all sharp edges and brief, brusque conversations. She barely noticed Luca or doorman Guido. When she did notice either man, it was to order him to fetch and carry.

Louise reminded Luca of his grandmother; troubled and aloof, waiting for people to leave so she could nurse her hatreds alone.

Perhaps she was the reason why Vito spent long hours at the club, either behind the bar or in his office. The uncrowned mayor of East Lido, he knew everyone, their spouses, and the names of their children. Residents came to him for loans, arbitration, and advice. Luca figured Vito heard more confessions than the priests at Saint Rocco's and resolved more differences than King Solomon.

Vito also taught Luca how to navigate Prohibition. Illegal beer deliveries from the Antonelli brothers were planned with care, using coded signals in telephone calls. More importantly, Vito knew which cops would take a payoff to reliably look the other way. Other cops, like O'Malley who patrolled their section of Hamilton Street, took Vito's money but couldn't be wholly trusted. And then there were those looking for an excuse to get Italians in trouble and call in the federal Prohibition Bureau. If that happened, arrests and confiscations would follow.

1920 turned into 1921.

Luca saw his first moving picture at Lido's Strand Theatre. *The Four Horsemen of the Apocalypse* swept the audience on an epic journey from Argentina to bloody battlefields in France and Luca was no exception. Vito never saw it, but virtually every other person in East Lido did. For weeks, Luca had to endure being compared to the smoldering Julio, played by Rudolph Valentino.

Teasing ended when the serious business of baseball came up. The Galliano Club team played in the Lido Industrial League. Tickets to games at Riverside Park cost 25 cents and teams got a portion of ticket sales.

Someone cracked that attendance would go up if folks knew the Galliano Club had a player who looked like Rudolph Valentino. As pressure mounted, Luca reluctantly joined the team only to discover the glorious counting game known as baseball statistics. He turned into a competent first baseman, which required ignoring legions of simpering girls draped over the infield fence.

The saloon was in an uproar for several nights in August when the first Major League Baseball Commissioner, a judge with the very American name of Kenesaw Mountain Landis, banned eight Chicago Black Sox players. They'd been acquitted in court of throwing the 1919 World Series against the Cincinnati Reds in exchange for a payoff from a gambling syndicate, but that didn't seem to matter.

The most heated discussions at the club that summer revolved around the trial of two Italian men in Massachusetts. The previous year, immigrants Nicola Sacco and Bartolomeo Vanzetti were arrested for a robbery and double murder. Now they were on trial. The *Lido Daily Clipper* breathlessly reported that they'd been found with guns, ammunition, and anarchist literature.

For weeks, evening debates swirled around the definition of anarchy and if anyone knew anyone who qualified as an anarchist. Luca listened without joining in, amazed at the freedom the members had to bellow such issues at the top of their lungs. He followed the trial closely, getting a firehose education in the American justice system. The two men were found guilty and sentenced to death. Calls for a new trial began almost immediately.

He tried to talk about the trial and its implications for the Italian community in America with Enzo and Rosaria, but their world was the farm and their growing brood of children.

Fear about anti-Italian sentiment crept into conversations in the club saloon as anarchist violence stayed in the news. After the verdict in the Sacco and Vanzetti trial, bombings occurred throughout the Northeast. The violence was attributed to the same Italian anarchist group called the *i Galleanisti* that had bombed New York City's Financial District in September 1920, killing dozens and injuring hundreds far from the neighborhoods Luca knew so briefly. *i Galleanisti* was the strong arm of Luigi Galleani, who was deported to Italy in 1919 for advocating the violent overthrow of the government and publishing a bomb-making book. Some club members were concerned that the name was too close to Galliano and American authorities would equate the two, but no one ever did.

Luca looked around Lido, comparing the endless opportunity there to the rigid society and dry dirt of Calabria, and decided that Luigi Galleani was a lunatic.

As 1921 came to a close, Vito surprised Luca on Christmas Eve with a promotion to bartender and bumped his salary to an astounding twenty dollars a week. In addition, Luca got his own key to open and close the club.

After everyone left that night, the two men headed for Vito's office. He worked the combination to the safe and extracted a bottle of wicker-jacketed chianti.

"My last." Vito filled two tumblers with the dense, fruity wine and lifted his chin at the wooden chair on the other side of the desk. "You're a good boy, Luca. You got a good head on your shoulders. A good mouthpiece, too, but you know when not to talk. People here like you. They respect you."

"Thanks, Boss." Luca accepted a glass and sat down, feeling the heavy brass key in the pocket of his wool trousers.

From his swivel chair, Vito beamed at him over the ledgers and papers scattered across the desktop. "*Salute*."

"*Salute*," Luca echoed, glass lifted for the traditional toast.

Vito swallowed his chianti in one long gulp and set about

refilling his tumbler. Luca looked around the office. He'd been in before, of course, to mop the floor and empty the ashtrays. It had the same masculine paneling as the saloon, which extended to a wall of built-in shelving behind the desk. The shelves were full of ledger books, yellow-spined National Geographic magazines that cost a whole fifty cents apiece, and assorted trophies won by the club's baseball and bocce teams.

Luca's eye was always drawn to the photographs. A large sepia portrait of a younger, thinner Vito standing next to a younger, happier Louise. Another of a baby in a christening gown. Smaller photographs in cheap cardboard frames were identified as relatives still in Italy by their ill-fitting suits and dark dresses.

Only one photograph perched on the desk instead of on the shelves. A young man in an Army uniform smiled at the photographer, dark hair curling tightly against his head. Puttees wrapped his calves and two medals adorned his chest. He held a campaign hat against his hip in a proud and rakish pose.

"Ciro." Vito saw Luca looking at the photograph. "Our boy who went to war with General Pershing."

"I heard that he was a good son."

Not long ago, a couple of club members told Luca why Vito refused to see *The Four Horsemen of the Apocalypse*. Ciro was just a kid when he answered the call and joined the Army. He died in 1918, chewed up by machine gun fire in a place called Belleau Wood.

"He never came back," Vito gulped down his second glass of wine. "Louise is still waiting. She hears him, she says."

"I'm sorry."

"He was older than you, but not by much."

"You miss him." Luca didn't know what else to say. He sipped his chianti and felt guilty because he no longer missed Rafaella. There was still grief, but the horrible hollow feeling was gone and he hadn't even noticed when it left.

"Ciro always wanted to be a soldier," Vito said, now on his third glass of the heady wine. "Did you ever want to be a soldier?"

"My father was a soldier," Luca said.

"What happened to him?"

"He died, too."

"In the war?"

"A different war."

"I have no son and you have no father." Vito gestured at Luca's empty glass. He refilled it and topped up his own. "We stay together, we'll be all right. Like family, no?"

Luca nodded. "I'd like that." They finished the chianti in silence.

Vito fell asleep on the sofa. Using his new key, Luca locked up and walked to Mrs. Esposito's boarding house, hands shoved deep in pockets and shoulders hunched against the cold. Stars twinkled overhead and moonlight cast a glow on the snowbanks piled up on either side of the streets. Icy snow crunched underfoot.

Enzo would pick him up tomorrow morning to spend Christmas Day at the farmhouse. Luca had gifts for everyone. Rosaria was a good cook and no doubt had prepared a feast.

Before climbing into bed, Luca took out the tin box that held the few items that were precious to him. His father's military portfolio, his own passport, the little passbook for his account at the First National Bank of Lido, and a book about

Saint Francis of Assisi from Father Caviglia. He opened the portfolio, extracted a strip of ribbon binding some papers, and threaded it through the hole in the top of the key to the Galliano Club.

The moment hit him hard. The brass key was the first tangible symbol that he belonged somewhere after so many years as an outcast. By adding his father's scrap of ribbon, he was somehow laying Matteo's ghost to rest.

He thought his father would have liked Vito Spinelli.

We stay together, we'll be all right. Like family, no?

Luca clutched the key, feeling its teeth dig into his palm. It was a good pain.

The Galliano Club was more than a job. It was a sanctuary, a refuge. A place where neither his sins nor his father's defined him.

It was home.

Nothing and no one was ever going to take it away.

PART 3: BENNY

March 1924

Basement of the Brewster Apartments, 2800 N. Pine Grove
Chicago, Illinois

Benny Rotolo wasn't the biggest slugger who worked for the North Side gang, but he had a flair for breaking legs. He was enthusiastic when it came to discouraging voters or busting up polling places, and the job sure paid better than picking pockets on Michigan Avenue.

It never made no difference who got elected mayor or alderman or head of a union anyhow. The gangs owned Chicago, not the politicians. The city was divvied up between Dean O'Banion's North Side gang, Johnny Torrio's Chicago Outfit, and the crazy Genna brothers in Little Italy.

Benny figured that tonight was his chance to move up. At 23 years old, he wasn't a kid anymore. If he didn't get busy, he'd be stuck in that fleabag apartment with his ma and her croupy cough forever. Not that she'd notice if he left. All she cared about was bathtub gin and the boyfriends who kept her in dresses and silk stockings.

The cavernous basement of the Brewster was dank and dim as Earl "Hymie" Weiss moved along the line of sluggers, paying them off for helping the boilermakers pick the right candidate as union boss. Littered with lead pipes, baseball bats, loose bricks, rake handles, and other tools of the slugger trade, the Brewster's basement often served as the rallying point for North Side troops. If the residents knew what was going on, they knew better than to complain.

Benny edged out of line and waited, cap in hand, real respectful. Hymie let everyone else leave before tossing a wad of bills in Benny's direction, along with a hard, appraising stare.

"You got moxie, kid," Hymie said. "I been watching you."

"I'm looking to move up," Benny said boldly, stuffing the wad in his pocket. He'd planned to say that, just like he planned what he was going to say next.

He'd either get a chance to prove himself, or be dead by midnight. Hymie Weiss was as ruthless and crazy as a starving junkyard dog. Kinda looked like one, too, with jug ears and a heavy Polish jaw.

"Every two-bit slugger wants to be a torpedo, kid," Hymie said.

"Every two-bit slugger isn't me," Benny replied.

Dead, unblinking eyes bored into Benny for an excruciating minute.

Hymie's real name was long and Polish. Woja-something. He might be taken for a boilermaker himself, with big, knuckled hands, a strong rangy frame stuffed into a newish suit, and those dead eyes set a shade too close together over a blunt nose. Enforcer and number two to Dean O'Banion, head of the North Side gang.

Volatile, ruthless, and entirely without remorse, Hymie Weiss was somebody to be reckoned with. The name alone sent folks running for the hills with their tail between their legs. It was no idle rumor but the honest truth that Hymie shot his own brother a couple of years ago. Left him for dead.

If Benny wanted to move up in the rackets game, Hymie

Weiss was the kind of fella who could teach him.

Benny licked his lips. "Somebody like you wants somebody like me watching your back."

Hymie snorted. "You know how to drive?"

"Sure," Benny lied.

"Come by Schofield's on State Street tomorrow at five o'clock with some wheels." Hymie swiped his mouth with the back of his hand. "We'll see what you're made of."

Benny dropped a ten-spot into his ma's lap when he went home and fell into bed. The next morning, he solved the driving problem by stealing a car. Nothing too eye-catching, just a black Ford that looked like every other black Ford on Clark Street, but with new Goodrich balloon cord tires advertised to be puncture-proof. Benny was sure they'd come in handy for whatever Hymie had in mind.

He managed to drive away from the downtown bustle and spent a couple of hours teaching himself to shift smoothly, accelerate like a getaway driver and turn without slowing down. The hardest thing to crack was how to stop quick and get going again without killing the clutch. Over and over, Benny sweated bullets as the Ford coughed and stalled. He still didn't have the knack by the time he put fifty cents worth of Sunoco in the tank, made his way to State Street, and parked in front of Schofield's Flowers.

Benny straightened his tie and tipped his hat and swaggered in like he belonged there. The florist shop was loaded with blooms in metal buckets and a real nice counter for taking orders. It smelled like a prissy girl's boudoir but Dean O'Banion ran the entire North Side bootlegging empire from the place. He made a tidy roll from the flower business, too, especially for services at nearby Holy Name Cathedral. Benny admired the way O'Banion made money on both ends. He knocked off his rivals and then supplied the flowers for their funerals. Fleeced 'em coming and going.

"Hey, kid." Clad in a nice brown suit with a skinny maroon tie, Hymie looked Benny up and down. A match bobbed in the corner of his mouth.

"This the new boy?" O'Banion was shorter and wider than Hymie, but a real Dapper Dan with a sprig of lily of the valley in the lapel of his jacket. Wide Irish face with thin lips and wispy eyebrows under neatly combed hair.

Hymie grunted. "We'll see."

"Pleased to meet you, Mr. O'Banion," Benny said. His handshake was returned, which was a good sign.

"Play it straight with Hymie," O'Banion warned. "He'll play straight with you."

Benny just had time to nod before Hymie muscled past the flower buckets and opened the door.

Outside, Hymie pointed to the Ford. "This yours, kid?"

"No." Benny figured he better tell the truth, like O'Banion said.

"Whose is it?"

"Borrowed," Benny said. "I didn't catch the name."

Hymie gave a raspy laugh and swung himself into the passenger seat.

Winter still nipped the air as Hymie told Benny where to go. Up one street, turn, drive down another, and on and on. Benny wasn't sure if Hymie was testing his talents as a wheel man or what, so he just did as he was told.

Hymie didn't exactly encourage questions. He was a

nervous passenger, with one heel jinking up and down against the floorboard. Something in his right pocket kept his hand entertained. The man continually scanned the street, eyes rolling in their sockets like marbles in a sock. Made Benny nervous, too, but mostly alert and excited.

"Pull over," Hymie ordered suddenly.

Benny braked hard. The front tire kissed the curb in front of the Majestic Theater. The motor died.

"Wait here." Hymie leaped out of the Ford and headed down the sidewalk, right hand in his pocket as he dodged pedestrians. A cop loitered on the corner of the next block. Cold sweat washed over Benny as it occurred to him that Hymie could knock off somebody right there and stick Benny in the neck for the job.

He watched as Hymie stopped and put an arm around a fella in an overcoat. They talked, real friendly-like. After a couple of minutes, they trotted over to the Ford.

Hymie opened the passenger door and leaned in. "Benny, this here is Tricker Egan. He's a pal. Gonna get supper with us at Nemo's Chop House."

"Sure, Hymie," Benny said, like he wasn't surprised at all. Nemo's Chop House was on the other side of the river. A steak there cost more than a 6-cylinder Cadillac. "Nice to know ya, Tricker."

"Likewise." Tricker was cut from the same cloth as Hymie. Shifty eyes and a ten-dollar suit. Nice overcoat though, the kind that hid a lot of hardware.

"Take the front seat, Tricker," Hymie said grandly and climbed into the back.

Benny got the Ford going again and set off in the general

direction of the restaurant. Hymie didn't tell him where to go, just acted like Benny knew. Hymie and Tricker started jabbering on about this fella and that fella and who owed who and whose trucks were delivering beer from the Sieben Brewery, a place O'Banion owned joint with Johnny Torrio, head of the Chicago Outfit. Torrio and his top lieutenant, a fatso named Al Capone, owned the rackets on the west side of Chicago.

In the middle of the conversation, quick as a crooked casino dealer, Hymie leaned forward and slipped a wire lasso around Tricker's neck. Cinched it tight, pinning Tricker's head to the front seat. Tricker's hat went flying as he gagged and flailed and kicked the dashboard and Benny, too. The Ford rocked from side to side. Benny struggled to hang onto the wheel.

"Keep driving," Hymie ordered, panting a little as he squeezed the wire.

Tricker reached inside his coat. Benny caught the movement out of the corner of his eye and threw out his right arm to keep Tricker from drawing.

Inside the coat, Tricker's gun went off like a bomb. Benny flinched and the Ford swerved. With Tricker gurgling and jerking as the slug tore through his leg, an oncoming delivery truck loomed out of the dark.

A horn blared, loud as the end of the world. Benny yanked the wheel in terror. The Ford ricocheted off the curb and shot back into the right lane.

Hymie switching from grunting to humming. Tricker went slack. His eyes stayed wide open, but he wasn't seeing a thing. The gun slid out from under his overcoat and clattered against the gear shift. Blood pooled on the floorboards of the stolen Ford.

Benny tried to breathe normal, like what happened to Tricker was no big surprise. He felt drunk. His head buzzed.

Hymie released the wire lasso. Tricker's body thumped against the passenger door, heavy as a sack of potatoes.

"Head west," Hymie ordered from the back seat. He wound up the wire and stuck it in his pocket. "We'll drop him in Cicero."

The Chicago Outfit owned the Loop, most of the South Side and neighborhoods like Chicago Heights, Blue Island, Burr Oaks, Stickney and Forest View, but Torrio and Capone had expanded into the western suburb of Cicero in a big way. They controlled the beer-running operation that supplied Cicero's saloons and ousted Eddie Vogel, a local politician who owned a chain of slot machines there. Joe Klenha, the mayor, was known to be in Torrio's pocket.

Like everybody else, Benny knew the joke. If you smell gunpowder, you must be in Cicero.

It didn't take a genius to know that Tricker had ratted out the North Side gang in some deal with Torrio and Capone. His body would be a message that the North Side knew what happened.

By the time they were approaching Torrio's speakeasy, the Four Deuces on South Wabash, Tricker's blood and guts were stinking up the Ford and Benny was addicted to the buzz in his brain. He wasn't sure how they were going to pull this off, what with the Four Deuces being Torrio's signature hot spot. Probably had twenty torpedoes guarding the place.

2222 South Wabash was a bulky four-story dark red brick

building with columns of bay windows flanking either side, making the place look like a castle that got started but ran out of moxie before the turrets got finished. The door to the club was right smack in the middle of the place, but Benny knew that the fake antique store on the left side of the first floor marked "A. Brown" was really Scarface Capone's private hangout. A recessed door on the far right was the entrance to a brothel. The Four Deuces had all those floors above the club for a reason.

"Slow down," Hymie said. As the Ford cruised up to the place, he reached over the seat and wrestled open the passenger door from the inside.

Tricker spilled partway out. Twisting behind the wheel, Benny aimed a boot at Tricker's backside and kicked hard. The body flew out the door and sprawled onto the sidewalk in front of the door to the club.

The motor of the Ford died.

A couple of Torrio's boys boiled out of place and scratched their heads like they didn't understand what they were seeing. Benny fought to get the Ford going again as they coasted along South Wabash with the passenger door flapping against the latch.

Just as the Outfit boys figured out that it was Tricker making a mess on the sidewalk, the Ford roared into life. Benny stomped on the gas, those balloon cord tires launched off the asphalt, and the Ford shot down the street just ahead of a hail of lead from a brace of Tommy guns. The Ford shimmied with the impact with a loud rattle and roll, but Benny hunched down and kept the pedal to the metal. Gravity shut the passenger door with a bang when he took a left turn on two wheels. Hymie laughed like a loon in the back seat.

They dumped the Ford as soon as they got back to Chicago and hopped on the "L" train back to State Street. The lights were off at Schofield's Flowers, but Hymie led Benny around the back and up a fire escape to the second floor. Dean O'Banion was there with a couple of primo members of the gang, including Vincent "Schemer" Drucci and George "Bugs" Moran who got his nickname because he wasn't exactly the most reliable thinker in Chicago.

The men were all in their shirtsleeves, drinking beer and playing cards. Some had their girls with them, all dolled up like real tomatoes and smoking cigars, too. Benny never saw a girl smoke a cigar before.

"Don't be looking for Tricker Egan," Hymie said. "He's busy keeping them entertained at The Four Deuces."

"I already got a call from Mike Merlo," O'Banion said. "Wanted to know if we was done. I told him maybe."

"Word travels fast," Hymie replied with a snort.

Even if they weren't Italian, everybody knew Mike Merlo. He was head of the Unione Siciliana, the big Italian fraternal society that kept a lid on the wops. Merlo was a big deal when it came to who was running Chicago. When the politicians who thought they ran the city complained about the Italians, he was the one they complained to, and when they needed Italian support for something, they came to him for that, too. When the Italian gangs fought with each other, Merlo brokered the peace.

And when Merlo wanted something for the Unione Siciliana, well, there were lots of folks who owed him.

"I said Egan was enough, for now. Besides he wasn't a

wop, so it wasn't Mike's problem." O'Banion nodded towards Benny. "How'd he do?"

"Fast thinker."

O'Banion gave a bloodless smile. "You in or out, boy?"

"In," Benny said.

O'Banion peeled a couple of C-notes off a fat roll and pushed them to the edge of his desk.

Hymie poured two beers from a pitcher. Handed one to Benny, along with the C-notes. "Buy yourself a new suit tomorrow," he said. "Hat, too."

Benny pocketed the cash, quaffed some beer, and joined in the guffaws as Hymie described his new system for getting rid of trouble and how Benny literally kicked the stiff out of the moving Ford.

It made for a good story. Hymie's gusto gave Benny an instant reputation as a tough guy, too. Not just a street slugger, but a real somebody in the North Side gang. Benny got a few toasts and lots of backslapping. Winks and cooing approval from the girls. Suggestions that he take a room at the Ambassador Hotel where some of the fellas lived.

By the end of the night, Benny knew the North Side gang was where he belonged.

November 1924

Schofield's Flowers, 738 North State Street
Chicago, Illinois

There wasn't much for Benny to do in the back room of Schofield's Flowers besides swill coffee and watch O'Banion fuss over a giant wreath for Mike Merlo's funeral.

Merlo, head of the Unione Siciliana, died two days ago. Everybody in Chicago with a drop of Italian blood in their veins was mourning him until they were blind drunk. No doubt that's why O'Banion's bodyguard Louis Alterie didn't show up that morning. Probably had a jackhammer of a hangover.

Despite the drinking and grieving, Merlo's death sparked uncertainty like a live wire hit by lightning. Nobody knew who was going to take his place in Chicago as the respected power broker both within the Italian community, and between the Italians and the rest of the city's stealers and shakers.

Nothing was going to happen until Merlo was buried, but Hymie was always thinking ahead and sent Benny to hang out at Schofield's until Alterie showed up again.

Benny poured himself some coffee from the fancy electric percolator. O'Banion hummed a bit as he clipped a few stems.

"Cup of tea, boss?" Benny asked and took out the kettle. There was always coffee for the boys but O'Banion liked tea.

Benny was rising through the North Side ranks because he paid attention to details. In fact, he was learning the smart end of the rackets business so fast it was like drinking from a firehose.

The North Side gang controlled dozens of breweries hidden in garages and basements and even more alky cooker operations making rotgut gin. The overall bootlegging operation was huge, with a fleet of trucks servicing speakeasies and saloons as well as the gang's gambling dens. Brothels practically minted money.

The gang's leg-breakers and sluggers collected percentages from freelance hookers, dope-dealers, fences who moved stolen goods, sharps running dice and stuss scams, and general street crime peddlers. If they worked North Side streets, they paid a tribute to Dean O'Banion.

Cash was the grease that kept Chicago's wheels spinning. The North Side gang paid stacks of bills to politicians and cops to look the other way, get sluggers out of the pokey if they got collared, and chase off Prohibition Bureau agents.

Hymie called it business. Benny called it the finest education a fella could wish for, especially when it came to collecting dough from the North Side's brothels. The girls always threw in a free ride for whoever came for the money, not that they had much choice.

Some of the brothels were real swank, with silk sheets and peroxide blondes who'd give a fella a massage if he'd been on a bender the night before. Benny liked the rough stuff, when the girls couldn't breathe and got all scared and bug-eyed. If they complained afterward, Benny made them regret it.

As much as he was learning, Benny was always sniffing the wind when it came to O'Banion and his uneasy collaborations with Johnny Torrio's Chicago Outfit and the crazy Genna brothers in their lair called Little Italy. Torrio had influence over the Genna brothers and was trying to be the big chief. Make the gangs work together, stuff like that.

In contrast, O'Banion always held out for North Side interests.

Torrio and O'Banion owned shares in each other's breweries, distilleries, and gambling dens. Things were smooth until a couple of months ago when the Genna brothers went beyond Little Italy and started marketing their whiskey in North Side territory. Benny was acting as Hymie's assistant and general factotum the day that O'Banion complained about the Gennas to Torrio. When Torrio didn't do anything, O'Banion exploded with rage.

Everybody knew something bad was going to happen.

A couple of weeks later, one of the North Side's snitches inside the Chicago police department told O'Banion that the cops were ready to raid the Sieben Brewery, one of the spots that O'Banion and Torrio owned together. With this juicy tidbit up his sleeve, O'Banion offered his shares of Sieben to Torrio. Said he wanted to sell out, leave the beer racket.

Torrio believed him and paid half a million for the shares. O'Banion took the money and went back to his flowers.

Cops raided the Sieben Brewery the next day. Closed it down and arrested Torrio and six of his sluggers. Torrio was hopping mad, knowing that O'Banion had outfoxed him. Like a chump who don't know when to quit, Torrio demanded his money back. Because he wasn't no chump, O'Banion refused.

Tension mounted, but last week O'Banion and Hymie went like always to the meeting at the Metropole Hotel with Torrio's lieutenants to tally up the week's profits and collect the North Side's cut.

Al Capone and Frank Nitti were there for Torrio.

Nitti was a runty older guy with a skinny mustache and nice suit pretending that he was the president of the First National Bank of Chicago. He had the reputation of being a hard man but a good planner and kept a low profile.

Benny figured Nitti was pretty smart. Capone liked the limelight. Easiest way to get dead in the Chicago Outfit was to steal either Capone's money or his thunder.

Like the other bodyguards and drivers, Benny waited in the hall outside the room where the big bosses smoked cigars and counted money. It was easy to eavesdrop because the walls were paper thin and Nitti's voice came through real clear.

"Angelo Genna's come up short this week," Nitti said. "But we have his marker."

"Nah." Capone's voice carried, too. "Cancel it. Professional courtesy."

"We're not running a charity for the Genna brothers." O'Banion's Irish lilt was equally loud. "He pays up, same as the rest of us."

The ensuing argument was swift. O'Banion didn't back down. With his ear pressed against the wall, Benny heard O'Banion make a phone call to Angelo Genna with the warning to pay up within the week.

Mike Merlo kicked the bucket a couple days later, taking the Unione Siciliana's thumb off the scales of gang rivalry.

Angelo Genna still hadn't paid his marker.

As the water heated for O'Banion's tea, Benny admired the wreath. It was enormous, a real fitting tribute kind of thing with a black satin ribbon adorned with *Rest in Peace* and enough carnations to choke a horse. Big arrangements of lilies and chrysanthemums waited to be taken to the church.

O'Banion had a real flair for funerals.

The bell over the door jangled a notice that customers were in the store. O'Banion told Benny to make the tea and headed for the front, limping a little like always because of a streetcar accident when he was a kid.

Benny turned off the hot plate and peeked around the doorway to check on O'Banion. A couple of well-known sluggers stood in the middle of the shop, looking around at all the pink and white roses. Frankie Yale, John Scalise, and Albert Anselmi were always where the action was in Chicago.

"Hello, boys," said O'Banion. He came around the side of the counter and held out his hand. "You from Mike Merlo's?"

Yale nodded and shook O'Banion's hand.

The handshake went on too long.

As Benny watched in frozen horror, Scalise and Anselmi pumped lead into O'Banion at point-blank range. Two bullets into the chest, two in his face, and two down his throat. Yale grimly hung onto the handshake, keeping his victim locked in place.

The stocky Irishman's body jerked with each shot. Chrysanthemums and roses trembled in their buckets. The plate glass window rattled.

When Yale released O'Banion's hand, the Irishman's bullet-riddled body crumpled to the floor.

The job done, Yale, Scalise and Anselmi legged it out of the shop and roared off in a big Cadillac, the kind favored by Capone and the Chicago Outfit boys.

Benny rushed to O'Banion. The North Side leader was a bloody, dead mess.

The next hour was a blur. Hymie put out the call for every

North Side top lieutenant to show up on the second floor of Schofield's. Nobody wasted time getting there.

He was taking over, Hymie announced.

Nobody had a problem with Hymie replacing O'Banion at the top of the ticket. Everybody knew he was the most ruthless among them and would orchestrate the North Side's revenge. It was equally obvious that Johnny Torrio was the stinking devil who ordered the hit on O'Banion in retaliation for the Sieben Brewery deal.

The last item on Hymie's agenda was hustling Benny out of Chicago. "If Yale finds out you saw," Hymie said. "You won't have time to shit your pants before one of them gets you."

"I don't want to go, Hymie," Benny argued. He was desperate to redeem himself. "I want to be the torpedo who gets Torrio."

Hymie snorted. "Listen to me, kid. You ain't fast enough yet for Capone or any other one of Torrio's goons. Find a place where you can lay low for a couple of weeks."

It was a hard pill to swallow, but Hymie was right.

"I got a cousin in Lido, New York," Benny said at last. "Works in a mill."

Hymie handed Benny a couple of C-spots. "Come back when we blow the all-clear."

Lido was smaller than a Chicago fart. The Italian neighborhood called East Lido was lousy with nuns and straight-arrow types. When the mill whistle blew, they lined up with their lunch pails to get in. His older cousin Nick Procopio was one of them.

Maybe being deputy foreman of the Lido Premium

Copper and Brass Rolling Mill was a big deal, but all Benny saw was his cousin coming home sweaty and dirty to a house full of squalling kids. There wasn't one betting parlor, speakeasy, brothel, or street gang in the entire place.

Every woman in Nick's neighborhood was a copy of the wife. Old country Italian with one eyebrow and snot-nosed kids clutching her skirts. Wouldn't dream of showing her ankles, bobbing her hair, or kissing a fella who wasn't her husband.

Nick and his friends escaped work, wives, and kids at a place called the Galliano Club not far from the mill. Benny went once with Nick.

Although it was big enough for a chorus line and a dozen bathtubs full of gin, the Galliano Club wasn't a speakeasy but a social club with sports pennants, a pool table, and a bar the size of a train car. The walls were decorated with photographs of the club's baseball team and the Lido Civic Band. No liquor, no girls, no music except for Enrico Caruso singing opera from a Victrola.

The owner was old and as fat as Capone. The barman was a Calabrian with an accent that a fella could cut with a knife. Looked like Valentino in *The Sheik.* Never cracked a smile but made a decent sandwich.

"Lido's the sort of place that's asleep at the wheel," Benny told Hymie as soon as he got back to Chicago. He'd hopped on the first train west as soon as the "all-clear" telegram arrived. "But a fella could really do something with that Galliano Club. Get a band and some girls in there for starters."

"You looking to move?" Hymie asked with a snort.

"Nah, there's nothing going on in Lido."

"Then shut up about home sweet home."

The second floor above Schofield's Flowers was Hymie's headquarters now, humming with high-voltage energy. Tommy guns were stacked in a corner, along with boxes of ammunition, cigarettes, and bootleg whiskey. Hymie's favorite torpedoes were there, including Schemer Drucci and Bugs Moran.

And Benny was there, too, glad to be out of a sleepy burg like Lido. Chicago was where the action was.

Hymie rapped the butt of his revolver against the desk and outlined how they were going to knock off Johnny Torrio.

Al Capone, too.

April 1925

South Wabash Avenue
Chicago, Illinois

Mabel Dooley wanted a new cocktail called a lemon drop, and right now Benny wanted whatever Mabel wanted.

She was a real classy tomato, with platinum blonde hair and skin so pale it was almost translucent. He always liked blondes, real or not, and mixed it up with plenty of them at North Side brothels, but Mabel was in a whole different league.

A real society type.

Her daddy owned a dozen shoe factories and gave his baby girl furs and jewelry and even a gray Marmon roadster with red trim that growled like a sulky tiger.

Benny met Mabel when she caught her heel in a sidewalk grating on Michigan Avenue and he yanked it out. His price for setting a princess free, Benny told her with his new pearly gray fedora tipped over one eye, was a cup of coffee. Mabel said she always paid her debts and let him carry her shopping bags into Swanson's Café like they owned the place.

Over coffee and banana cream pie, Benny gave her the razzle dazzle about owning a company that imported chocolate from Switzerland. Mabel batted her eyelashes and cooed that it sounded wonderful. She'd always wanted to go wherever that was.

The gimmick worked every time. Dames loved chocolate.

Tonight was their second date and he was behind the wheel. Mabel wasn't quite drunk enough for the rough stuff

Benny had in mind for later in his room at the Ambassador Hotel, so he steered the flashy Marmon south. With a couple of gin fizzes under his belt, he felt bold enough to suggest that they hit the Four Deuces. Torrio was still in the hospital after Hymie filled him full of lead a couple of months ago in retaliation for O'Banion's death. The place belonged to Capone now, lock, stock, and barrel.

Ever since he and Hymie dumped Tricker Egan's body in front of the place, Benny wanted to go inside the lion's den. He could bring Hymie some inside dope on the place, too. The Marmon was just the vehicle if a quick getaway was in order.

Besides, maybe Capone had a bartender who knew how to make a lemon drop cocktail.

A real strong lemon drop cocktail.

Mabel's dress sparkled like liquid silver all the way to her ankles and the fox around her shoulders was the genuine article. Benny felt real swell in his pearly fedora with his name embroidered on the satin lining, and matching topcoat over a double-breasted penguin suit from Marshall Field's on State Street. The jacket had a special pocket for his hefty Colt, padded so that nobody could see that he was carrying.

With the parked Marmon getting envious looks from punters up and down the sidewalk, Benny tipped the doorman 20 smackeroos and Mabel glided into the place in that rich girl way of hers. He tipped the hat check kitten to take care of the coats, then led Mabel to a table where he could check out the place with his back to the wall and his eyes on the door.

It wasn't no dump, that's for sure. Lots of dark paneling, linen-skirted tables, and crystal chandeliers. A jazz band was playing, competing with laughter and drunken chatter. The dance floor was awash with couples in evening dress. A waiter came by and assured Mabel that he'd bring her a lemon drop. Benny ordered another gin fizz.

Benny didn't recognize anyone there, although the blue haze of cigarette smoke blurred every face beyond the crowd at the next table. Mabel lit up and massaged Benny's knee with her free hand. He grinned and winked at her.

The waiter brought their cocktails and a bowl of pretzels. The lemon drop looked like yellow motor oil in a champagne coupe, a sprig of mint balanced on the rim. Mabel immediately took a big swallow. Her eyes widened as the poison went down the hatch.

"It tastes like medicine," she giggled. "Lemony medicine."

"Let me taste," Benny said.

Mabel made to slide the coupe to him, but Benny leaned over the table and stuck his tongue in her mouth. At first, she tried to draw back but he clamped a hand around the back of her neck. Mabel relaxed and slid her hand up his thigh.

"Nice," Benny said when they came up for air, his voice husky.

She giggled again and sipped at the lemon drop.

A wide shadow darkened the white tablecloth just as Benny was about to take a slug of the gin fizz. It was Al Capone himself, hefty and sullen with slick hair, a faultless tuxedo, a diamond pinky ring, and those distinctive scars raked across the left side of his face.

"You a little lost sheep tonight, Rotolo?" Capone asked in that Brooklyn whine of his.

"Hello, Capone," Benny said, flattered to be recognized

despite the danger. He lifted the gin fizz in a toast to his host. "Nice place you got here."

"Introduce me to your friend," Capone said as his eyes undressed Mabel.

"Mabel, this is Mr. Al Capone," Benny said reluctantly. "This is his place. Capone, this is Miss Mabel Dooley. Her daddy runs Dooley's Fine Footwear."

"Miss Mabel Dooley." Capone took Mabel's hand and pressed it to those clown lips of his. "A real pleasure. As Rotolo said, this is my place. You come to me if you want a good time."

"Pleased to meet you, Mr. Capone." Mabel turned on her high beams. "I've read about you in the newspapers."

"Sure, you have." Capone's big paw was still stuck to Mabel's as he leered at her shimmery bosom. "I'm a businessman, serving the needs of the public. Nothing wrong with that, is there?"

"None at all," Mabel purred. "That's why Benny brought me all the way across town. Said if we could find a lemon drop cocktail anywhere, it would be here."

"No kidding?" Capone dropped Mabel's hand, snapped his fingers and two thugs in penguin suits materialized behind him. "Come all the way across town for a reason, Rotolo? Weiss send you?"

Before Benny could move, one thug twisted him into a headlock. The other reached inside Benny's jacket and extracted the Colt as well as a set of brass knuckles.

"Benny!" Mabel exclaimed as Benny gasped for air. She turned to Capone, drunkenly earnest. "He sells chocolate. Everybody wants to steal his recipes."

Capone and the thugs roared with laughter. Benny's vision started to blur.

"Chocolate!" Capone wound down, mopping his eyes with a silk handkerchief. "Jake and Vinny, meet the chocolate king! Does Weiss know you got a sideline?"

"Listen--." Benny gasped.

The pressure of the thug's arm around his throat lessened and Capone grabbed Benny by the lapels, lifting him out of his seat. "You go back to Hymie Weiss and let him know we know he done in Angelo Genna in retaliation for the hit on O'Banion. The Genna boys ain't gonna take that lying down. Weiss is gonna pay, same as he's gonna pay for the hit on Johnny."

Angelo Genna had been killed in his flashy roadster on Ogden Avenue two weeks ago. A sedan pulled up next to him on the street and unloaded a Tommy gun out the window. Genna swerved into a lamppost, wrecking his vehicle and busting up his spine. His funeral was a real spectacle. The procession to Mount Carmel Cemetery included the crumpled roadster, towed along for a truly unique expression of gangster grief.

"You want to send a message to Hymie, do it yourself," Benny snarled breathlessly.

Capone's meaty fist walloped into Benny's midsection. He doubled over and threw up those last two gin fizzes.

"Take him for a ride," Capone ordered, thrusting Benny back into the arms of the two thugs.

"My Marmon," Mabel exclaimed.

To make his humiliation complete, one of the thugs found the key to the Marmon in Benny's pocket and gave it to Mabel. As his fedora was mashed down over Benny's eyes and the thugs muscled him away, he heard Mabel tell Capone that she was such a ninny to have believed Benny's story and could she please have another lemon drop. Capone promised to help her recover from the shock.

A Cadillac waited behind the club. Benny was tied up, gagged, and bundled into the trunk. The car stopped hours later. Jake and Vinny hauled Benny out, untied him, and spun him until he was sick.

As the retching eased, Jake yanked Benny upright. Both thugs had big revolvers in their hands.

"We'll count to three before we start shooting," Vinny said.

Clutching his pearly fedora like it was going to save him, Benny looked around dizzily. They were on some godforsaken country road, well outside Chicago. Between the edge of the road to a wooded area was a clearing at least 20 yards deep.

"One," Jake said softly.

Benny took off running, slipping on the muddy ground in his leather-soled shoes. Bullets whizzed past. One took a bite out of his sleeve. Another clipped his heel, sending him sprawling flat. Momentum and panic rolled him through a patch of weeds and then he was up again, zigzagging as if possessed, distant laughter spurring him on.

Splinters rained from a tree as he gained the woods, stinging his face. With his heart going like a jackhammer, Benny blundered his way deeper and deeper into the woods, desperate for a place to hide.

He was well and truly hidden by springtime foliage when he heard doors slam and the Cadillac drive away. Benny leaned against a tree and sucked in a deep lungful of cold morning air.

His hand shook as he touched his cheek and felt warm blood.

The sun was high in the sky and burning away the dew by the time he dared to return to the road. A rickety truck with a farmer behind the wheel picked him up as he held out his thumb.

"Car broke down, young feller?" the farmer asked.

"Something like that," Benny said.

With the precious fedora jammed on his head, Benny sagged against the door of the truck. He'd get Capone if it was the last thing he ever did.

PART 4:

WELCOME to LIDO

April 1925

601½ Hamilton Street
Lido, New York

Ruth slowly pivoted, taking in the big empty room. The newspaper advertisement called it a storage space. Three walls were finished plaster, but the fourth was exposed brick, with iron water pipes and heat ducts running across the top. Afternoon light streamed through the windows overlooking the busy street below, but two electrified chandeliers waited for evening.

Her heels clicked on the wooden parquet floor as she crossed to the single interior door. Opening it, Ruth saw the latest in indoor plumbing, including a toilet with a pull chain, a pedestal sink, and a claw foot bathtub.

The one-bedroom apartment on the other side of the stair landing had the same amenities.

On hour earlier, when Ruth came to see the so-called storage space, Mr. Spinelli refused to believe she wished to rent it and guided her instead across the hall. He and his wife had recently moved out of the cozy apartment and would rent it furnished. Despite Ruth's best efforts to make him understand she was interested in the storage space across the hall, he kept pointing out the things that came with the small apartment. A full-sized bed. A small dining room table and four chairs. Chintz curtains that his wife had made herself.

"You don't want this place," Mr. Spinelli said. He waved a hand at the brickwork and the emptiness.

"It's perfect," Ruth said.

"Heat, yes." He held the door open, waiting for her to walk out. "But no kitchen, no furniture. It's no good for a nice lady like you."

Like everyone else in this neighborhood, her potential landlord was Italian. Ruth guessed he was in his late forties, with sad eyes, a soup-strainer mustache, salt and pepper in his dark hair, and a paunch that strained the buttons of his vest.

He ran the Galliano Club, a social club for men, which took up the entire first floor of the blocky two-story brick building on Hamilton Street. It presided over a sprawl of Italian-owned businesses, shops, and restaurants. Ruth liked the noisy energy of the neighborhood, the maple trees budding with spring, and the mouth-watering smell of coffee and sugar coming from the nearby Bella Napoli Pastry Shop.

This could be where she remade her life.

"Maybe I could rent both," Ruth ventured. "The apartment to live in and this storage space for a dance studio."

"Dance studio?"

"A school," Ruth explained. "To teach children to dance. There isn't one in Lido."

The jail in Poughkeepsie had given Ruth plenty of time to plan her future. She had gone back on the road in another vaudeville show until she could implement the plan, but it was more than she could manage. The iron constitution necessary for the grueling performance schedule was long gone. The miscarriage and major surgery had stolen her health and it would take time before she was truly well again.

As for another kind of job, well, who would hire a woman with a prison record?

When the vaudeville show came to Lido, she knew it was the right place. Lido had no school of dance but was big enough to support one. The small city was growing and needed all sorts of new goods and services. Even better, Ruth didn't know anyone there and no one knew her.

Neither the Varsity Sisters nor Ballroom Expressions with William and June Wilson had ever performed in Lido.

There was just one kink in her plan. Ruth had exactly thirteen dollars to her name.

"Both." Mr. Spinelli pulled at the end of his mustache as he mused the situation. "Thirty-five dollars a month for both."

"With heat and water?"

"Sure."

It was an excellent price but still too high. Ruth looked critically at the unfinished wall. "Thirty for both," she countered with more confidence than she felt. "I'll give you ten now for the first month and the rest as soon as I have students."

That left her three dollars to hire a piano and someone to play it, advertise in the newspapers, print up flyers to hand out, and feed herself until she got students.

The mustache quivered. "Maybe nobody comes to dance."

"I'll give you and your wife dance lessons for free, too," Ruth said a little desperately. "Private ballroom dance lessons. She'd like that, wouldn't she?"

"No." Mr. Spinelli tugged at his mustache again. "You

speak good English, no?"

Ruth blinked at the unexpected question. "Well enough."

"I think we can make a deal," Mr. Spinelli said slowly. "Thirty dollars a month for both and you teach English to Luca in the morning, before the club opens."

"Luca? Is that your son?"

A shadow passed over the man's genial face. "No, Luca works in the club."

"Deal." Ruth swiftly opened her purse and pulled out two precious five-dollar bills. Luca was probably some thick-headed lunk, but if it meant getting both the apartment and the studio space for a bargain price, she'd hammer a whole dictionary into his head. "We can start his lessons tomorrow morning."

Mr. Spinelli held out the keys. "Thirty dollars," he verified. "Luca can carry your things upstairs. Then we sign the paper. Yes?"

"Yes, to make it official." Ruth's fingers closed around her future.

Mr. Spinelli shook his head sadly and handed back one of the five-dollar bills. "You can't start a business with nothing. Pay me twenty-five at the end of the month."

"Thank you," Ruth breathed. Getting five back meant she had eight dollars. It was enough for everything and some dinner, too.

She fetched her suitcase from the downtown hotel and lugged it all the way to Hamilton Street, beaming the entire time. Lido was her city now and she was Ruth Cross, soon to be the proprietress of Tapping Toes School of Dance, 601 ½ Hamilton Street. When she could afford it, she would have business cards printed up and go to Chamber of Commerce meetings.

Sweating from the long walk, Ruth plunked down her suitcase in front of the Galliano Club building. Vito had given her a ring with three keys, but there was no indication which key belonged to which lock. It took two tries before she unlocked the street door emblazoned with 601½ on it. Before she could push the door open and head upstairs, a man popped out of the club door to the right.

"I can help you," he announced, the Italian accent softening the end of every word.

"Are you Luca?" Ruth asked.

"Yes, I'm Luca." He pressed a hand to his heart to indicate himself. "Luca Lombardo."

"I'm Ruth Cross. I've rented all of the upstairs from Mr. Spinelli."

"Welcome." He pointed to her suitcase. "You have more?"

"No, just this." Ruth showed him the keys. "Mr. Spinelli and I made a bargain. As part of my rent, I'm to give you English lessons."

"Thank you." He hesitated. "I wish to know more words in English."

Obviously, he was no thick-headed lunk. There was a serious aura around him, a self-contained mantle that Ruth found both unusual and attractive.

The sleeves of his band-collar shirt were pushed up to reveal forearms bulging with ropy muscle. Light brown hair fell across a high forehead but was cut razor short at the sides and neck. He was perhaps 10 or 12 years younger than her, yet his eyes were old.

She knew he'd seen hard things. Perhaps he'd been a soldier.

"We'll start tomorrow," Ruth went on. She smiled encouragingly. "In the morning."

"I will make coffee," Luca said without returning the smile.

"Coffee. For the club?"

Luca pointed to Ruth. "You teach English." He pointed to himself. "I make coffee."

"Oh, for the lesson." Ruth expected that he would be a quick study. "You'll make coffee when I come to give you the lesson. That's very nice. Thank you."

"*Si*. Coffee."

She smiled again. "Mr. Spinelli said to meet at ten o'clock before the Galliano Club opens. We can study at the table by the window. Can you meet me in the Galliano Club then?"

"I will meet you in the Galliano Club."

"Wonderful."

Luca picked up Ruth's suitcase and started up the stairs to the second floor. Ruth followed, watching his back muscles ripple under the smooth cotton of his shirt as he shifted her suitcase from his left hand to his right.

Ruth decided that he was better looking than Rudolph Valentino, Douglas Fairbanks, and Ramon Novarro all put together. Put him in a suit and tie, teach him to smile, and he could own Broadway.

He deposited her suitcase in the tiny parlor and left Ruth alone to marvel at her situation. Her luck was finally changing. She had enough in her purse to launch the Tapping Toes School of Dance, a furnished apartment all to herself, and a new name. Pirouetting to the window, she looked down on Hamilton Street. Automobiles trundled in either direction, under the watchful eye of an electric streetlamp that would provide a comforting pool of light at night. There were shops of every size and description in either direction.

She checked out the tiny kitchen and dining room before peeking into the bathroom. The indoor plumbing was nicer than any hotel, and it was all hers. No more shared washrooms in cheap hotels.

The bedroom was as snug as the rest of the place, with a brass bedstead, a rocking chair, and a built-in closet with cunning niches for shoes and bags. Everything Ruth owned would fit with plenty of space to spare.

The bedroom window overlooked a gravel lot behind the building that merged into an alley running parallel to Hamilton Street, bordered by a line of maple trees. The big black roof of a touring car occupied half of her view and she guessed the vehicle belonged to her new landlord.

Ruth sank into the rocking chair and closed her eyes. For the first time in forever, she felt like she was home. No one in Lido knew about Poughkeepsie. The Galliano Club was a friendly place, a brick bulwark that would protect her as she started her new life.

Nothing bad would ever happen here.

May 1926

The Galliano Club, 601 Hamilton Street, Lido, New York

The Galliano Club had two rules. No cheating. No fighting.

It wasn't a rule, but everyone knew that Vito would carry a member on the books for up to six months if they ran into financial trouble, longer if a sick kid was involved. After that, a delinquent member either had to start paying their dues or resign.

Since coming to work for Vito, Luca had become adept at refereeing arguments and knowing when a drunk needed to be shown the door. But only one member was actually tossed out for violating the rules. A Sicilian by the name of Filipo Morello started a melee in the pool room when he nudged a ball into a pocket with his thumb. Things got so bad that Luca had to wade in with the Commodore baseball bat he kept behind the bar. It came all the way from Dickson, Tennessee, where they apparently grew sturdy trees. The bat performed as well against thick-headed Sicilians as it did against southpaw pitchers.

Flung out of the Galliano Club's front door and into the

middle of Hamilton Street, Morello staggered home to beat his wife. She fought back with a cast iron frying pan. Five days later at his funeral, she hid her bruises under a black lace mantilla.

All the married members of the Galliano Club were subdued for a month. Lorenzo Bastico's flower stand sold out.

The club was doing a brisk business on this balmy spring evening. The Lido Premium mill blew its closing whistle early on Saturdays and didn't reopen until Monday morning, making Saturday the one night in the week when every member headed to the club. Luca had tapped a fresh cask of beer that afternoon in anticipation of a full house. The Antonelli brothers still supplied the club, driving down from Canada every few weeks, and the cellar was stocked with beer as well as the legal low alcohol near beer and fizzy tonics from the Utica Club brewery.

Under the Yankee pennants pinned to the wall opposite the bar, two tables of card players were intent on games of pinochle. A group clustered around a marathon chess match prolonged by beer and tall tales. Members drifted in and out of the pool room where the weekly tournament meant nickel bets, scattered applause, and ivory balls clacking loud enough to be heard over noisy conversations in the saloon.

Cigar smoke blued the air as Luca ranged up and down the bar, filling glasses, ringing up sales, dishing out pickled eggs, and adding a word here and there to conversations. Drinkers at the end of the bar closest to the window planned the Galliano Club baseball team's strategy. They were the favorite in the Lido Industrial League but in the first game of the season, the Teaberry Knitting Mill team trotted out a batter who hit two triples and a home run against the Galliano Club's pitcher, costing the club the game. From first base, Luca had watched in envy as the Teaberry player sent the ball soaring over left field again and again.

On the other end of the bar, the conversation was all about the headline splashed across the evening edition of the *Lido Daily Clipper:*

BYRD POLAR FLIGHT ACHIEVES HISTORIC RECORD

Lieutenant Commander Richard E. Byrd (U.S. Navy, retired) and civilian pilot Floyd Bennett flew over the North Pole, beating the competition and stunning the world. Articles about the historic flight, complete with photographs and diagrams, filled every column inch below the big headline.

Coolidge Congratulates Byrd on Polar Flight

Story of Byrd's Flight from Brooklyn Over Top of World

Byrd Did in One Flight All He Had Planned

Byrd's Great Fokker Machine

"Big day for America, eh, Luca?" Jimmy Zambrano asked and held up his empty beer glass. Leaning on the far end of the bar, Jimmy was the well-respected foreman at the Lido Premium mill. Nearly 50, with a wiry build, a Roman nose, and closely cropped dark hair fading to gray above his ears, Jimmy was one of Vito's closest friends.

"Flying over the North Pole." Luca expertly filled the

glass from a pitcher of beer and mentally added fifty cents to Jimmy's tab. "Hard to imagine flying over miles and miles of ice."

"Atlantic City was far enough for me." Next to Jimmy, Luca's cousin Enzo nursed his beer and scanned the newspaper.

Enzo made an appearance at the club once or twice a month, always on a Saturday night. When the club closed, Luca would go back to the farm with his cousin, spend the night in the attic, and on Sunday help Enzo with chores that required an extra hand. Tomorrow they'd start the back-breaking task of clearing land for a new barn.

"Speaking of Atlantic City," Jimmy said to Luca. "Vito talked about taking Louise somewhere. Did he mention it to you?"

"No." Luca glanced at Vito playing pinochle at one of the card tables, glad to see the boss was still sober and in good spirits. "But it would be good for them to take a vacation."

Vito's grief at losing his son was getting worse as time went on. Beer and whiskey, when he could get it, took the edge off what Vito had taken to calling his "blue dog days."

Those were the days when Vito stayed in his office, mired in drunken gloom. Blue dog days gave Luca more and more responsibility for keeping the club running and solvent. Doorman Guido Serra helped, but he got confused if asked to do much more besides greet members and shovel snow. It didn't take long before Jimmy and others close to Vito knew that Luca was running the club but everyone maintained the polite fiction that Vito was still in charge.

Jimmy moved away from the bar. Enzo picked up the

newspaper and showed Luca a diagram of the North Pole flight. "What makes a man do something like that?"

"Maybe he wanted to be first."

Luca tried to imagine himself in an airplane with the roar of engines filling his ears instead of the mix of Italian, Sicilian, and Calabrian voices that circled the saloon. Byrd and Bennett had flown a round trip from Spitsbergen, which was somewhere north of Norway, in a huge tri-motor Fokker airplane christened *America*. Veteran explorer Roald Amundsen, conqueror of the South Pole via dogsled, was also in Spitsbergen preparing a flight over the North Pole in the Italian-made dirigible *Norge*. Despite delays and hardships, Byrd triumphed and won the air race to the North Pole.

Luca poured himself a tonic and read the tri-motor's specifications with interest. It was 42 feet, 9 inches long with a wingspan of 63 feet and 3 inches. Two 100-gallon tanks were carried in each wing, with two additional tanks of 110 gallons each in the fuselage. The engines drank 28 gallons of fuel an hour and had a top speed of 117 miles per hour. The flight lasted 15 hours and 30 minutes.

Before Luca could calculate the distance between Byrd's base in Spitsbergen and the North Pole, a commotion erupted across the room. Vito boiled out of his chair at the card table. "Procopio, I want to see your hand!"

Another card player bolted to his feet. His chair overturned and hit the floor with a crack as loud as a gunshot.

"I got nothing to show you, old man," Nick Procopio snarled.

"I'm asking you with respect, Nick," Vito said.

Nick thumped his chest with a fist. "You calling me a

cheat?"

"With respect," Vito repeated hotly.

"Show your cards, Nick," added one of the still-seated players.

Conversations about the North Pole and baseball trailed off. Members lining the bar two and three deep turned as one. Pool players hovered in the mouth of the hallway.

The saloon lapsed into an ominous quiet. Tobacco smoke swirled noiselessly to the ceiling.

A big brute of a man with hands like shovels and a voice tuned to be heard over pounding machinery and molten metal, Nick was Jimmy's deputy at Lido Premium. He had the neck and shoulders of a bull as he loomed over Vito, who was a head shorter and twenty years older. Vito's vest buttons strained across a belly that grew more ample every year.

Nick lowered his head, the better to glare at Vito. "You saying I cheated?"

The saloon throbbed with tension; the other pinochle players frozen in their seats. No one had ever challenged Vito like this before. Luca backed away from the bar until his hand closed around the Commodore bat in its usual spot by the work counter.

"Prove me wrong or get out," Vito said, his mustache quivering in anger. "You know the rules."

"Not my rules, old man!" Nick grabbed the table with both hands and heaved.

Luca vaulted over the bar as precious glasses of beer and wine lofted into the air, along with a confetti shower of pretzels and pickled onions. Everyone on that side of the saloon scrambled to get out of the way. Chairs scraped against the floor and overturned. As the pinochle deck of cards and half a dozen glasses rained down, the upended table crashed to the floor hard enough to rattle the pictures on the wall. The lights over the bar flickered.

Nick threw a wide looping punch at Vito that went wide as the Commodore smacked into the deputy foreman's elbow and caused him to lurch sideways. Luca followed up with a swing worthy of the Teaberry Knitting Mill that connected with the man's ribs. Nick cannoned into the wall and doubled over.

The fight was over as quickly as it began.

Helped by Jimmy and Enzo, Luca hustled Nick past a stupefied Guido and out the front door. Cool night air cleared hot heads as they gained the sidewalk outside the Galliano Club. A few automobiles rumbled past on Hamilton Street, but there was nothing remarkable about four men having a chat outside the well-known hangout.

"Go home, Nick," Jimmy said quietly, a hand on Nick's massive bicep. "Sleep it off."

"Not your fight, Jimmy," Nick growled. His breath stank like sour beer, but even drunk he didn't challenge Jimmy's quiet authority.

"You're out, Nick." Luca held the bat held across his chest in both hands. "You know the rules. I'll refund your dues for the month."

Nick wrenched himself away from Jimmy and spat in fury. The gobbet of saliva landed at Luca's feet. "You tell Spinelli that Nick Procopio don't forget."

"Go home, Nick," Jimmy said again.

Nick snorted and staggered away, one hand pressed to his

ribs.

They watched him go until he turned left into the warren of narrow streets north of Hamilton Street.

Luca hoped Nick's wife had a cast iron frying pan.

Overhead, a canopy of stars competed with streetlamps on both sides of Hamilton Street. The glow illuminated the signs of shops up and down the street. Like the mills, most would be closed until Monday.

Six blocks away, the gold crucifix on top of Saint Rocco's steeple glinted in the moonlight.

Enzo was the first to speak. "Jesus. Nothing like this ever happens on the farm."

Luca gave a shaky laugh.

"You're a good man in a fight, Luca," Jimmy said and rubbed Luca's shoulder with a work-roughened hand. "You got somewhere to be tomorrow?"

"I'll be at the farm with Enzo," Luca said. "Why? Do you think Nick will come back?"

"I'll talk to him on Monday," Jimmy said. "Square things with him. You take care of Vito."

"Sure." Luca knew what Jimmy really meant was *don't let Vito drink himself to death over a card game.*

"Jesus," Enzo said again.

They went back into the club, which was abuzz as everyone told everyone else what they'd seen from their vantage point by the bar or the vestibule or the hallway to the pool room. Luca got a cheer and a dozen reenactments of his batting technique. There was general agreement that Nick had cheated and deserved to lose his membership, although the stigma was considerable, especially given his lofty status as deputy foreman of the Lido Premium mill.

Despite the clamor, Luca got tables and chairs righted, and the pinochle games and chess match resumed. The tournament in the pool room wound down as balls clicked together in rapid succession. Luca refilled his pitchers from the cask under the bar, rang up another fifteen dollars' worth of the Antonelli brothers' fine Canadian beer, rehashed the North Pole flight, shrugged off his prowess with the Commodore, and worried that the boss was headed for another blue dog day.

At closing time, Vito patted Luca's cheek, told Enzo goodnight, and left without saying a word about the encounter with Nick Procopio.

Enzo was still wound up as he drove Luca to the farm around midnight. As Luca fell into bed in the attic, he heard muffled voices coming from below. Enzo had woken Rosaria to recount the evening's big event.

It was times like this that Luca missed having a wife next to him, listening to his version and telling him that he did the right thing and that she was proud. Instead, he was living like a priest. The irony gnawed at him.

The years were passing, but Luca wasn't willing to settle for the women East Lido had to offer. An endless supply of sisters and cousins just arrived from Italy, with long skirts and kerchiefs over their hair, who knew how to cook and clean and pray and produce children but not how to read, write, or add a column of numbers. They were all versions of Rafaella and afraid of this new place called America.

He wanted something different; a woman who wasn't tied to the old ways. A woman who wanted more.

But he couldn't shake the fear that Rafaella and their child had died as punishment. After murdering Orsini, Luca had compounded his state of mortal sin with the sacrament of Holy Matrimony in the church. He could confess and be granted absolution if he truly felt remorse. But he did not.

The only thing Luca ever stopped counting was the number of times he'd prayed for absolution nonetheless.

As a result, he would not marry in the Church again and what Italian woman would agree to that? Besides, how could he afford to marry when half of his salary went to the Bank of Napoli every month?

The familiar refuge of the counting game beckoned. Assuming the tri-motor's top speed of 117 miles per hour for the entire duration of the flight, Lieutenant Commander Byrd and pilot Floyd Bennett had flown over 1800 miles of icy wasteland from Spitzbergen to the Pole and back. But if the airspeed of the tri-motor varied, the distance covered would change. What if they flew at 110 miles per hour for the first hour, dropped to 90 miles an hour for a period, then increased to the maximum for 30 minutes, and so on? What about wind? Had that made a difference? The calculations of speed and distance were infinite.

Below him, Enzo and Rosaria ended their whispers and were quiet. Luca finally fell asleep wondering if Byrd and Bennett had someplace to call home, the way the Galliano Club was home for him.

September 1926

West Monroe Street
Chicago, Illinois

As he strolled toward the Majestic Theatre, Benny tipped the pearly fedora with his name sewn into the lining over his left eye. Every girl on West Monroe Street would look twice. Once for the hat, a second time because Benny's dark hair and blue eyes had that effect on dames. The huge sign for the theater, visible from blocks away, advertised a new revue. He'd catch a matinee later.

Word got out last year about Benny's run-in with Capone but instead of Hymie killing him for going to the Four Deuces, Benny earned some grudging North Side respect. His version of the truth made all the difference. As Benny told it, he bought Scarface Capone a drink in the man's own establishment, just to show that the North Side gang couldn't be intimidated. Gave Capone a lesson in swagger and style.

Benny never mentioned the ride to the countryside or how close he came to getting shot in the back by Capone's enforcers. In his version, Mabel had fucked him dry afterward, too.

Since then, Chicago streets had only become more dangerous. Johnny Torrio never came back from Italy after being all shot up and the Unione Siciliana was no longer the big power broker. War with Capone's Chicago Outfit was hotter than Hades.

Capone unleashed Jake "Machine Gun" McGurn to gun down the rest of the Genna brothers. After a couple of misses trying to avenge O'Banion's murder, Hymie was planning an all-out assault on Capone's headquarters.

Millions in bootlegging and brothel revenues were at stake and neither side was going to give an inch when it came to territory or booze. Capone's reputation was growing, small players were after the Genna brothers' revenue from Little Italy territory, and the cops were all wildcards. Some were paid off; others were still honest. Sometimes it was hard to tell one kind of cop from another. Prohibition agents were upping their game, too, with a new intelligence unit moving into Chicago that was supposed to be incorruptible.

Earlier in the year, Hymie did a couple of weeks in jail and came out swinging, more volatile and brutal than ever. He'd lost a little weight, too, and there were rumors he had the cancer. Everybody stepped careful around him, wary of his wild unpredictability.

Street shootouts were all too common. In July, Hymie and Schemer Drucci were attacked on Michigan Avenue in the middle of the day. Twice.

Benny had a new Colt Pocket Hammerless automatic in his right pocket, a short-barreled shotgun hidden inside his cotton trench coat on the other side, and 600 dollars in his wallet. The money was his pay for busting up a couple of saloons near the Hawthorne Works factory. The owners needed to be persuaded to buy their beer from the North Side instead of the Chicago Outfit.

In between persuasion jobs, Benny was still one of Hymie's drivers. He also delivered beer, acted as a lookout, collected money from brothels and bootlegging operations, and encouraged local politicians to vote the North Side way. But when Hymie went to jail, Schemer Drucci and Bugs Moran edged Benny out of the innermost inner circle. Rumor had it that they didn't trust him because of his connection to O'Banion's murder.

Benny was looking for the right opportunity to prove his loyalty, something flashy that would make Hymie include him in the big attack on Capone. The plan was for an armada of cars to drive up to the Hawthorne Hotel, Capone's new headquarters, and blast it to bits. Benny pictured himself aiming a Tommy gun out a car window and letting loose with a fusillade of lead that exploded windows and turned Scarface Capone into a sieve in a silk suit.

Mabel Dooley, too, if she was with him.

He whistled at a couple of real tomatoes that passed him on the sidewalk in cloche hats and fur jackets, their high heels tapping like an invitation. They giggled in response but continued on their way. Benny decided not to follow them. There were better pickings in Hymie's brothels. Those girls didn't complain when Benny got rough because he always paid extra to get extra.

"Hey, Benny!" Lefty Wilcox caught up to him, coattails flying. His signature white feather fluttered in his hatband.

"Hey, Lefty," Benny said, slowing down. "What's your hurry?"

Lefty was a legbreaker a couple of rungs below Benny on

the North Side ladder. No genius, but he was famous for taking the rap when Hymie punched a girl right in the kisser. Lefty went to the can for six months, but never squealed.

"Jesus, Benny, haven't you heard?" Lefty's eyes darted up and down West Monroe Street, where cars and buses engaged in another day of free-for-all Chicago traffic.

Benny frowned. "Heard what?"

"Capone knows that it was you what busted up his saloons the other night," Lefty said. "The Outfit's put out a contract on you."

Benny grabbed the lapel of Lefty's coat and hustled him across the sidewalk to the shelter of the closest building. "Who told you that?"

"Everybody knows," Lefty said, jerking away. "Word on the street is that Capone's offering two grand and something called a lemon drop."

"I must be fucking important," Benny quipped, but his mouth went dry. Two thousand dollars to rub him out was twice the going rate and the lemon drop gag was a direct message to him.

"Capone's got Frank Nitti looking for you." Lefty rocked back and forth on the balls of his feet, making the feather tremble in agitation. "Those saloons had to be coining money for him."

Frank Nitti wasn't just a money man, then. Benny recalled the older man's humorless and calculating silence. It was the perfect cover to be Capone's chief enforcer.

"You'd better not go back to the Ambassador," Lefty went on, naming the hotel where they both kept rooms. "They've got the place staked out."

"Yeah, sure." Benny scanned the street, mentally racing through his options. "Thanks for telling me."

"You take care," Lefty said and held out his hand. "Everybody wants Capone's two grand."

The ex-con's handshake came with an iron grip. It took Benny a beat to realize that Lefty wasn't letting go, just like when Frankie Yale killed O'Banion. That beat was enough time for Lefty to dip his shooting hand into his coat pocket.

In a move he practiced every day, Benny kicked the ready shotgun under the trench coat into his free hand. He blasted a hole in Lefty's chest, absorbing the booming recoil.

Lefty blew backward like a tattered rag doll, hand levitating out of his pocket. A big dogleg revolver clattered to the sidewalk. When Lefty hit the pavement, Benny gave him the other barrel just to make sure.

A woman screamed, horns blared, and men shouted. A police whistle cut through the mayhem. Benny hid the shotgun under his coat again, still attached to the stout hook sewn into the lining. The barrel was hot against his side as Benny took off running, scattering terrified pedestrians in front of the Majestic like pigeons.

He sprinted around the corner, right into an ambush. Lefty had set him up, not once, but twice. Two bulbous Cadillacs, the Chicago Outfit's signature bulletproof ride, roared straight at him. Men with Tommy guns balanced on the running boards. Those Chicago typewriters rattled out an arc of bullets that slammed into the building as Benny winged by. Bits of stone chipped off and stung his cheek.

Benny hurled himself into the first open doorway and kept going. He was in a men's clothing store, a swanky maze of tweed jackets, silk ties, and glass cases full of folded shirts. A place to hide but also a potential trap.

"Where's the back door?" Benny barked as he swiftly reloaded the shotgun.

There were two clerks in the store. The one closest to Benny had white hair, a stiff collar, and a look of frozen terror plastered over his mug.

Outside, tires screeched and doors slammed.

Benny grabbed a black fedora from a display and swapped it for his pearly one.

"Excuse me," the clerk quavered.

Benny pumped two rounds from the Colt Pocket Hammerless into the old geezer, blundered through a curtain into a storage room, and hit the back entrance. He emerged into a loading zone for the row of shops running perpendicular to West Monroe and one of Frank Nitti's teenaged torpedoes.

The shotgun move cut the kid down in a spray of blood and buckshot. Benny hightailed it out of there, knowing the rest of Nitti's crew would not stop to help their fallen comrade. He kept up the pace, sucking air, the shotgun weighing him down, until he found an "L" station and jumped onto the first train that stopped. His coat was spattered with blood. Other passengers turned away in fright as the elevated train roared and rattled over the raucous city below.

Benny rode the trains for an hour, constantly switching cars and directions, until he was sure he wasn't being tailed. As the adrenaline ebbed, he knew he had to get out of Chicago. Capone's big bounty meant that even North Side pals could not be trusted. Meanwhile, Nitti would be relentless. For a Chicago Outfit hood, killing in Capone's name was a matter of honor.

It was getting dark. Benny got off at the new Union Station, praying that Nitti hadn't positioned his torpedoes there. With the stolen fedora jammed down to his ears and his heart thundering, Benny sauntered through the Great Hall like he hadn't a care in the world. Nobody leaped from the barrel-vaulted skylight or took a potshot from behind one of the huge marble pillars. Timetables showed a train leaving for Buffalo in an hour, enough time to buy a one-way ticket and the dinner special in the Harvey House restaurant.

He sat with his back to the wall and eyes on the entrance, but there was no sign of danger. The food came fast and hot, delivered by a real kitten of a blonde waitress in her white Harvey House pinafore. He tucked into the tenderloin steak sandwich with gusto, stuffing the grilled onions back in with his fingers when they slithered out after a bite.

From Buffalo, he'd catch the train to Lido on the New York Central line. His cousin Nick would hide him until things cooled down in Chicago. Lido was the perfect spot. Capone would never look for him there.

Lido was tiny compared to Chicago but it had potential. It was smack in the middle of New York between the Mohawk River and the Erie Canal and crammed full of working stiffs like his cousin who pumped copper and brass out of the big mills. Lido was small enough to know everybody who was anybody, yet big enough to make things happen. Benny never thought about it before, but all that industry meant easy money and thirsty men. The location was prime, too. Goods moved in and out of Lido on the river, the canal, the railroad and rural roads that went all the way up to the border with Canada.

The Harvey House waitress came back, flashed a dimpled

smile, and asked if he wanted another cup of coffee. She was a real blonde, not the bottle kind like Mabel Dooley. If she looked that good in a white pinafore, she'd probably look like a million bucks in a silver gown and a fox coat.

Benny gave her his cup and a wink, feeling a surge of optimism. He had outwitted Al Capone, who probably had Frank Nitti staked out in front of the Ambassador, freezing his nuts off.

The fresh cup of coffee was hot and strong. A smart fella could own a place like Lido the way Capone owned Cicero. Benny could build a rackets empire stretching across upstate New York, with operations from Buffalo to Albany, and all points in between. Beer, hard liquor, hookers, extortion. Everything Hymie Weiss had ever taught him.

He'd have his own version of the Four Deuces, too. Take that club where his cousin Nick played cards and turn it into the finest speakeasy east of Chicago. Benny drummed his fingers against the tablecloth as he tried to remember what it was called.

The Gallo Club. No, the Galliano Club. Sure, the Galliano Club, on account of that big bottle of yellow liqueur behind the bar. He pictured the place in his mind's eye, but with a jazz band and a crush of dames and gents, all slurping gin and putting money in Benny's pocket.

Champagne, crystal chandeliers, and a floor show. Girls upstairs turning tricks. All he needed was some seed money and a place to brew beer.

And a blonde on his arm.

Benny caught the waitress's eye. He lifted his cup to signal that he needed a refill.

JOIN THE READER LIST

Never miss a new release! Sign up to receive exclusive updates from author Carmen Amato.

Go to: carmenamato.net/mystery-ahead

NEXT IN SERIES

MURDER AT THE GALLIANO CLUB

Luca Lombardo is the jack-of-all-trades at the Galliano Club, a hangout for Italian mill workers. He'll do whatever it takes to keep it afloat, including staying silent about a murder in the alley behind the club.

From her second-floor window, Ruth Cross witnessed the murder, but a scandalous past keeps her quiet.

Could hitman Benny Rotolo be involved? Run out of Chicago by Al Capone, he longs to add the Galliano Club to his own burgeoning bootlegging empire.

The longer the murder at the Galliano Club goes unsolved, the bigger the web of lies will grow. Not everyone will get out alive.

Turn the page to read an exclusive excerpt >>

MURDER AT THE GALLIANO CLUB

Chapter 1

By the time Benny Rotolo was in Lido for a week, he had a plan, a partner, and a line on a patsy with access to big money. As he waited in the Model T, twilight faded to evening and Benny reflected on what a swell education Chicago's North Side gang had given him. Dean O'Banion. Hymie Weiss. Bugs Moran. In their own way, each had taught him how to find a man's weak spot.

Lido was right smack in the middle of New York state, just north of the Mohawk River, and duller than dishwater. Summer nightlife meant a dance at Saint Rocco's church, a lecture at the Women's Institute, or a Buster Keaton picture at the Strand Theatre. Six years into Prohibition, too, like nobody knew how to take advantage of a good thing.

A smart fella could step into empty shoes, so to speak.

Benny squirmed a bit in the passenger seat of the Model T, trying to find a more comfortable position for the Colt Pocket Hammerless concealed in the inner breast pocket of his sixty dollar suit from Marshall Field's. The wool suit had been right for windy Chicago but upstate New York's summer humidity turned it into a steam bath.

They were parked in the lot next to the huge Lido Premium Copper and Brass Rolling Mill, which stretched into the night for two city blocks. Five stories tall to accommodate the giant block-and-tackle machinery that moved crucibles of molten metal and stamped out copper sheeting for ship hulls and who knows what else. The black-framed windows sheathing the enormous building glinted in the moonlight. Compared to the mill, the single-story brick Lido Premium office building on the other side of the lot was no bigger than a shoebox. A light was on in one of the offices, as well as over the entrance.

The mill faced Hamilton Street in the section of the city known as East Lido. At this time of night, any road in Chicago would be clogged with cars and buses and people heading to the next good time, but not here. Benny could see a sliver of the street from where they were parked and it was mostly quiet.

East Lido was home to Italian mill workers like his cousin Nick Procopio who lived crammed into the warren of narrow streets above Hamilton Street. At this hour of the night, those chumps were playing cards at a neighborhood fixture called the Galliano Club six blocks away.

Nick used to belong to the Galliano Club, but not anymore. That suited Benny just fine; meant Nick was available to go into business with him.

Behind the wheel of the Model T, his cousin produced a hunk of cheese and half a loaf of crusty bread from a wrinkled napkin. The smell of ripe provolone thickened the night air.

"You got to eat now?" Benny demanded.

"I worked twelve hours today," Nick said and held out a fistful of food. "You want some?"

"Jesus, Nick. No." Benny waved the cheese stink away. "You sure Fisher works late every Friday, all by himself?"

Benny had asked the question a dozen times. The situation was too good, too easy.

"I told you. I seen the night watchman's logs."

"You think Fisher's dipping his hand into the petty cash?"

Nick grunted and chewed. "What else would he be doing?"

Deputy foreman of the Lido Premium mill, Nick was a bull of a man, with shoulders that jutted like twin cliffs, hands the size of iceboxes, and a pumpkin head that sat directly on his shoulders. A frayed bandana was tied around the spot where his neck should be, distracting from a grease-stained canvas shirt, dirty dungarees, and the steel toed boots he wore to the mill six days a week.

Benny's cousin might look like a roughneck and be saddled with a horse-faced wife and four snot-nosed kids, but Nick was smart enough. When Benny appeared on his doorstep, having fled Chicago one step ahead of Al Capone's enforcer Frank Nitti and his trigger-happy torpedoes, Nick didn't flinch. Not only that, but he helped Benny make a plan and identified this Fisher fella as somebody who could be persuaded to help.

Slouched against the passenger door, Benny adjusted the Colt again and thought about dames. The blonde he'd picked up on the way out of Chicago was old news. Too prim. Meanwhile, East Lido was a bastion of Italian wives with one eyebrow and mewling kids.

But with a little more folding money in his pocket, blondes would find Benny. His dark hair, blue eyes, expensive clothes, and confident swagger attracted them like bees to honey and made their clothes fall off.

"He turned out the light." Nick gulped down his last mouthful. The low brick office building was dark now except for the entrance.

Benny watched as a slight figure in a suit and fedora came out and paused under the light to put a key in the lock. The fella looked to be ten years or so older than Benny, maybe 35 or 36 years old. A plain face but dressed real swell. Tailored suit with a faint chalk stripe and a red bow tie, same color as a silk one Benny had thrown away. White handkerchief in the breast pocket. Polished shoes.

A signet ring glinted as he locked the door. Somebody liked expensive things.

Obviously unaware that he was being watched, Fisher scurried toward another black Ford, the only other vehicle parked in the lot. Nick and Benny met him halfway.

"Evening, Mr. Fisher," Nick said.

Fisher gave a start and backed up a pace. "Ah, Procopio," he said. "The whistle blew hours ago. What are you doing here so late?"

"Need to talk to you," Nick said, looming over the smaller man.

"Can't it wait until Monday?"

"I brung my cousin."

Benny stuck out his hand, real friendly. "I'm Benny Rotolo, Nick's cousin."

"A pleasure to meet you. I'm Owen Forbes Fisher, the accountant for Lido Premium." Fisher shook hands, evidently relieved to see that Benny wasn't another mill worker like Nick. Clearly admired the swell suit, as well as the black fedora that Benny had lifted from some bespoke men's shop on his way out of Chicago.

"I've got a business idea," Benny said. "Nick here had a

notion that you could help us get it off the ground."

"If this is related to Lido Premium," Fisher said, looking from Benny to Nick and back again. "Speak to Henry Blick on Monday. He's the operations manager."

"No, this is more up your alley." Benny moved closer. "You being a money man and all. I could use your expert investment advice."

"Expert investment advice?" Fisher preened a bit.

"Exactly." Benny rubbed his hands together. "What would you say to becoming a potential investment partner in a business with a guaranteed two hundred percent return?"

Fisher's eyes nearly popped out of his head. "Two hundred percent?"

Benny nodded. "I'm from Chicago. Looking to set up a Chicago-style business. A partner with some seed money to invest could recoup their investment in thirty days. Even less. Everything after that is money in your pocket, free and clear."

"There is only one business with a return like that," Fisher said.

"That's right," Benny agreed, still real friendly. "The beer racket."

"No, no," Fisher protested. "I can't help you with anything like that."

"You got a nice position here, I take it." Benny cut his eyes to the office building. "But you're still driving yesterday's Ford. Bet you'd like a La Salle or a Packard. Bet you got a wife who likes nice things, too."

"Yes." Fisher swallowed hard, making his Adam's apple jump like a champagne cork. "Cynthia."

"She like pretty things?"

"Yes."

"Guaranteed two hundred percent return," Benny emphasized.

Fisher dabbed at his upper lip with the white hanky from his breast pocket. "I don't have any money to invest."

"Nobody's expecting you to invest your own money." Benny pointed a thumb towards the office building. "Not when this place is lousy with it."

Unaware of his own move, Fisher's free hand pressed on his jacket pocket to keep it closed.

Guilty. The best kind of patsy.

"We need cash and equipment," Benny went on. "A couple hundred more or less, plus the kind of equipment you order for the mill. Nick can tell you what to get. You place the order and square it with the books. Me and Nick can handle the rest. See? Nothing too complicated."

"I'd be stealing from my employer."

"Borrowing," Benny countered.

"Stealing," Fisher repeated, trying to sound indignant. "You want me to steal. Fake receipts and cook the books."

"You're doing it now," Benny said coolly. "What's the difference?"

Fisher's face twisted in alarm. "Who told you that?"

Quick as a wink, Nick smacked away Fisher's hand, allowing Benny to find out what was hidden inside the pocket. He pulled out a couple of folded bills and nearly laughed. "Ten dollars! In Chicago you can't even get laid for ten dollars."

"That's mine," Fisher gasped. "It's none of your business."

"You take it out of petty cash?"

Fisher's chin dimpled like he was gonna cry. "Cynthia wants a mink jacket."

"What else does she want?" Benny stuffed the bills back into the other man's pocket. "Take the same risk for our little business proposition and you could buy her the moon."

"You don't understand what you're asking," Fisher whined. "A brewery needs industrial equipment like chemical tanks. Hoses. Pumps. Heating coils. It's an expensive proposition."

"See." Benny said to Nick. "Man knows what he's talking about. Just the partner we need."

"I'd have to perform miracles of accounting to hide paying for it all."

"But you know how," Benny said leadingly.

"False receipts. Changes to inventory accounting. And the quarterly report. No, it's impossible."

"Two hundred percent return on investment," Benny reminded him.

Fisher plied the handkerchief against the sweat on his forehead. "Exactly where would this equipment go?"

"The old mill that burned down." Nick crowded into the conversation. "On the river below the Settlers Rest cemetery. The pumphouse is still standing. Can't see it from any road."

"The old mill?" Fisher was agog. "That riverfront property belongs to Lido Premium and the Packham family."

"Nobody goes there," Nick growled.

"But they could."

"Then you'll see that they don't," Benny said.

Fisher's face was shiny with sweat. "An illegal brewery at the old mill. Dear Lord."

Benny grinned; the hook was in the fish's mouth. "Nick and I will handle customers and delivery. We need cash for trucks and payroll until the beer sales start rolling in. Won't take long. Lido is lousy with fellas who want a beer when the whistle blows and even more that don't want to work in a mill no more."

"We'd be partners?" Fisher dabbed some more. "The three of us? Splitting profits three ways?"

"Sure." Benny stuck out his hand. The man was hooked. "Shall we shake on it?"

"I need some time to think about it," Fisher said but he extended a limp paw. "But in any case, I want the arrangement in writing and signed by all of us."

"Sure, Fishy," Benny said.

Benny reeled him in the next night when they met up at Perk's Diner, a rough spot on the south side of Lido. Sandwiched between the freight railyard and a scrap heap, it was the kind of place that served soup and sandwiches to teamsters and stevedores. A blue neon sign advertised *Fresh Coffee 24 Hours*. A row of Fords nosed against the side of the building.

Fisher was out of place, darting glances at the rough customers and fidgeting with excitement. Benny knew the feeling, knew what was going on in the accountant's head. Fisher was scared at the notion of being in the beer racket, but it put some steel in his spine, too. He was going to be a rich gangster, not just some mealy-mouthed bean counter scamming petty cash.

They ordered coffee and pie. Fisher produced a brand new business ledger book covered in gray linen with maroon corners. Benny wrote "The Lido Outfit" on the flyleaf and they all signed their names. Then they got down to business and hammered out the details. The equipment and supplies needed to be delivered fast.

Fisher took the ledger book with him when he left Perk's. Maybe the accountant thought it was some kind of insurance policy. Benny didn't care. The only insurance he needed was the Colt Pocket Hammerless.

Through the plate glass window, Benny watched Fisher get in his Ford and rattle off across the gravel. "Got us a new pet, Nick." He grinned at his cousin. "A dog who comes when ya whistle and all it took was writing names in a book."

Nick grunted and shoveled in some pie.

Benny dug into his own slice, the plans in his head getting bigger and bigger. Al Capone's Chicago Outfit had put a price on Benny's head. But in six months Benny was going to have enough money and firepower to spit in Capone's eye.

Once the beer racket was up and running, other rackets would follow. Protection, brothels, gambling. Benny would own money-making joints from Buffalo to Albany. Own the cops everywhere, too, starting with Lido. Just like in Chicago, but cheaper by the dozen.

Benny would rule his rackets empire from the finest speakeasy in New York. The Four Deuces on Wabash Street in Chicago was a shack compared to what Benny had in mind.

A floor show with a chorus line, gambling in the back, lottery sales, and girls turning tricks upstairs. Red velvet everywhere. Crystal chandeliers. A bar as long as Hamilton Street. Cocktails the size of punchbowls.

Torpedoes with Tommy guns to keep the riffraff out. A

road in back for quick getaways.

Benny was just about to tell Nick about the place he had in mind to become his new speakeasy when two blondes walked into the diner. One of them gave Benny an appraising look that melted into a slow smile and he lost his train of thought.

ABOUT THE AUTHOR

Carmen Amato turns lessons from a 30-year career with the Central Intelligence Agency into crime fiction loaded with intrigue and deception.

Her award-winning Detective Emilia Cruz mystery series pits the first female police detective in Acapulco against Mexico's drug cartels, government corruption, and social inequality. Described as "A thrilling series" by National Public Radio, the series includes CLIFF DIVER, HAT DANCE, DIABLO NIGHTS, KING PESO, PACIFIC REAPER, RUSSIAN MOJITO, and NARCO NOIR.

Fans of international mystery and police series by Ian Rankin, Jo Nesbo, Ann Cleeves, Peter May, and Jussi Adler-Olsen, as well as Don Winslow's cartel and border thrillers set in Mexico, also love Detective Emilia Cruz's complex plots, fast action, and exotic location.

The series was awarded the Poison Cup for Outstanding Series from CrimeMasters of America in both 2019 and 2020 and has been optioned for television.

Originally from upstate New York, Carmen was educated there as well as in Virginia and Paris, France, while experiences in Mexico and Central America ignited her writing career.

She has been a judge for the BookLife Prize and Killer Nashville's Claymore Award and is a recipient of both the National Intelligence Award and the Career Intelligence Medal.

Learn more at carmenamato.net

Made in the USA
Middletown, DE
29 July 2022